THE CLAYBURN COURIER

GLORIA'S GOSSIP

June 2007

Tongues are wagging and history is repeating itself. What offspring of which notorious retail king has been seen dallying with the daughter of said retail king's onetime paramour? Are our eyes deceiving us, or is the heir to a department store dynasty truly making a play for the progeny of his mother's arch-nemesis?

Are the fireworks real? Or is the millionaire playboy only playing footsie toward some darker end? Stay tuned....

Dear Reader,

Though I wasn't at the national romance writers' conference where the idea for this series was first hatched, I was lucky enough to be asked to work with authors whose names I knew, whose books I'd read and whom I aspired to be like. What a thrill!

I had a blast writing Kelly and Ryan's story, and hope you enjoy reading it as much as I enjoyed writing it. Kelly is the daughter of the town sexpot, Ryan the son of the town's wealthiest philanderer. Their parents had an adulterous affair. Now, though, can this former bad boy and former good girl who are determined *not* to be their parents possibly find a future together?

Enjoy!

Anna

ANNA DePALO

AN IMPROPER AFFAIR

Published by Silhouette Books

America's Publisher of Contemporary Romance

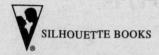

SILHOUETTE BOOKS

ISBN-13: 978-0-373-76803-5
ISBN-10:   0-373-76803-6

AN IMPROPER AFFAIR

Printed in U.S.A.

Books by Anna DePalo

Silhouette Desire

Having the Tycoon's Baby #1530
Under the Tycoon's Protection #1643
Tycoon Takes Revenge #1697
Cause for Scandal #1711
Captivated by the Tycoon #1775
An Improper Affair #1803

ANNA DePALO

discovered she was a writer at heart when she realized most people don't walk around with a full cast of characters in their heads. She lived in Italy and England, learned to speak French, graduated from Harvard, earned graduate degrees in political science and law, forgotten how to speak French and married her own dashing hero.

A former intellectual property attorney, Anna lives with her husband and son in New York City. Her books have consistently hit the Waldenbooks bestseller list and Nielsen BookScan's list of Top 100 bestselling romances. She has won a *Romantic Times BOOKreviews* Reviewers' Choice Award for Best First Series Romance, and her books have been published in over a dozen countries. Readers are invited to surf to www.desireauthors.com and can also visit Anna at www.annadepalo.com.

For my aunt Angela Dagostino, and
my editors, Melissa Jeglinski and Jessica Alvarez

One

Cooling his heels in a backwater like Hunter's Landing wasn't Ryan's idea of a good time, but then, nothing was these days.

He was so close to victory he could almost taste it, and since revenge was a dish best served cold, he intended to take his time savoring the triumph.

In the meantime, he didn't intend to let his prey off the hook. Webb Sperling—CEO and chairman of the board of Sperling department stores, and the man he was forced to call his father—would never know what hit him.

Now he walked along one of the main shopping drags around south Lake Tahoe, keeping his eye out for a place where he might pick up a wedding gift. If he was stuck in Hunter's Landing for the month of June, he might as well figure out what amusements lay nearby.

There were precious few amusements to be had in Hunter's Landing itself, that was for sure. He figured the locals in such a quiet little place depended on their cable service for access to television, the Internet and the world.

Cable interested him. *Cable* had made him rich. His company, El Ray Technology, was among the bigger players in California's fabled Silicon Valley.

A store sign hanging from a metal bar up the street caught his eye. Distressed Success, it announced in flowery type.

His lips curved in sardonic amusement.

The sign summed up his life.

When he drew even with the store, he was able to see it was a tidy little shop devoted to home furnishings. Its facade was white with light blue and yellow trim, like an Easter egg, and both its store windows presented cozy tableaus of domestic bliss.

The window on the left showcased a table set for tea with mismatched cups and saucers. The table had a distressed finish and was covered with a chintz tablecloth and set for four.

The window on the right displayed an old-fashioned settee—something that looked as if it had been salvaged from a garage sale—strewn with an outrageous assortment of silk, beaded and tasseled pillows.

It was domesticity with a hint of sin, he thought, his gut tightening.

The look would have suited a room tinged with Eastern exoticism—or a madam's boudoir. Here, on the California border with Nevada, where regulated brothels were legal in some localities, the decor would have found a ready market.

Intrigued by the storefront, he decided to have a look inside.

A chime above the door announced his entrance.

"These raw-silk photo albums just came in last week—"

The woman's voice, with just a hint of huskiness, washed over him, along with the faint scent of a flowery blend.

He walked around a display table and came face-to-face with the owner of that voice.

She glanced up, smile in place, and he felt the air leave him as if he'd taken a sucker punch to the stomach.

Hello.

"Good afternoon…"

Her voice trailed off as they stared at each other.

He went tense, the elemental reaction of a male who's gone too long without a mate.

He looked at her hand, noticed she wasn't wearing a ring and felt his spirits lift.

Things were looking up for his enforced month-long stay in sleepy Hunter's Landing, he thought bemusedly.

Tall and curvaceous, she had hair that flowed past her shoulders in loose curls. He had to call it titian colored, for lack of a better word.

She was a latter-day Venus—a model for the goddess of love that would have made even Botticelli proud. She had a pale heart-shaped face and symmetrical features.

She was dressed in a brown velvet top, ruffled skirt and high-heeled sandals. The look was professional but with a hint of the bohemian, and it dovetailed with the image of her shop.

She stood with a well-dressed, middle-aged female customer, the two of them flanking a waist-high white counter upon which were arrayed a number of albums.

She cleared her throat and righted the smile that had wavered. "Please take a look around and let me know if you need anything."

She hesitated a second, as if she belatedly realized how the words could be interpreted, and he felt his lips twitch.

"I'll be able to assist you as soon as I'm done," she said.

He thought about how he'd like her to *assist* him and smiled with lazy assurance. "No problem. Take your time."

She looked momentarily uncertain, then turned back to deal with the customer in front of her.

The mood broken, he sauntered around the shop, at the same time taking the opportunity to study her.

Over the years, he'd had plenty of confirmation that women found him attractive. Still, his charm was rusty from lack of use. His last relationship—if a three-month fling could be called that—had ended nearly a year ago.

Her voice reached him from the back of the shop. "These are interleaved with acid-free pages—"

He eyed a floor lamp with a tasseled flower-print shade, then a wrought iron chandelier with beaded glass strands of blue and green.

He felt as if he'd entered a fantasyland, one with a profusion of colors and textures.

Still, her shop couldn't compare to her. *She* interested him as no woman had for a long time.

"—we also have some leather-bound albums you might like—"

Her voice caressed his mind like the stroke of a petal.

He'd definitely been too long without sex, he thought. *Too long without anything except work.*

And now, thanks to his old college buddy Hunter—who'd gone to his grave too young—he had too much time to think about it.

At Harvard, he and Hunter and five other guys had formed a small band—a fraternity unto themselves.

One night, across a table strewn with beer bottles, they'd vowed to make their own marks on the world, though they'd come from families of distinction and wealth. They'd vowed to come together again in ten years to celebrate their friendship and success.

But shortly before graduation, Hunter's sudden and shocking death from melanoma had ripped the group apart, and they'd eventually lost touch.

That is, until a few months ago, when he and the remaining Seven Samurai had gotten letters from a Los Angeles law firm representing the Hunter Palmer Foundation.

Before his death, Hunter had apparently made arrangements for a lodge to be built near Lake Tahoe, and now, reaching from beyond the grave, he expected his friends, as they reached their milestone decade past graduation, to honor the vow they'd made to one another.

By the terms of Hunter's will, if each guy spent a month at the lodge, at the end of six months, twenty million dollars would go to charity and the lodge itself would be bequeathed to the town of Hunter's Landing so it could be used as a restorative place by cancer survivors and patients.

Twenty million was a lot of moola, and not even Ryan, hard-hearted millionaire that he was, could say no.

So that was how he found himself in this predicament. He was trapped in Hunter's Landing at the precise moment he was closing in on the goal he'd worked years to achieve—making Webb Sperling pay and then pay some more.

His mouth twisted. Of course, leave it to Hunter to find a place called Hunter's Landing for his old college buddies to serve their time. Hunter had always had a peculiar sense of humor.

Three guys had gone before him to the lodge, Ryan thought, so they were already halfway through this ordeal.

Of course, all three of his old buddies had somehow managed to get themselves engaged or married, including Devlin, whose month at the lodge had just ended.

In fact, Ryan had shown up in Tahoe early—and had stayed at a casino last night while the caretaker was having the lodge cleaned in anticipation of his arrival—because Dev was getting married tomorrow and had asked Ryan to be his best man.

Ryan grimaced. Devlin had even referred to the lodge as the Love Shack.

Right.

He eyed Venus again. He'd settle for a good lay, since that alone would be a vast improvement over his recent love life.

"I hope you enjoy your purchase."

Venus's voice broke into his thoughts.

He glanced around to see her walking her customer to the door.

A jangle of bells marked the customer's departure and Venus paused to organize a display of books. Silence heralded the fact that they were alone.

He watched her line up the spines of some books and then adjust the angle of a photo frame.

Finally, after what felt to him like aeons, but what was certainly no more than a few moments, she looked up and fixed him with a smile.

"May I help you?" she asked, walking toward him.

"Looking for a wedding gift," he said. "I was passing by and the name of your shop made me curious."

"A lot of people have had the same reaction," she admitted. "The name's served as a good advertisement for the shop."

"You're a savvy marketer."

This close, he could see her eyes were hazel beneath perfectly arched brows. Her lips were full and glossy pink, her complexion creamy and unblemished. It was hard not too be knocked over by so much perfection.

"Thank you." She seemed to consider him. "Our style aims for shabby elegance so—"

"Shabby elegance?" The name wanted to make every male cell in him snort in derision. "That's an oxymoron if I ever heard one."

"Yes," she responded, "but it's also part of a hip trend—one of its hallmarks being furniture with a distressed finish."

"And here I thought the name of your store was a description of my life."

She laughed.

He liked her laugh. It had a musical quality to it and he wondered if he could get it to a huskier timbre in bed.

He lifted a clock from a nearby shelf, checked the price and raised his eyebrows. "People are willing to spend a lot of money to look poor."

She nodded. "Celebrities included." She added with a light laugh, "This *is* Tahoe, after all."

"There's a market for expensive mismatched china?"

"Yes," she confirmed, refusing to look the least bit insulted. "It's an art form to bring together disparate pieces to create a harmonious look. I'll hunt for something a client is looking for if one of my regular suppliers doesn't have it."

He supposed more than one customer had been seduced by Venus's sales pitch. "Any suggestion for a wedding gift for a couple that already has everything?"

His question brought a smile to her lips. "Young couple or old?"

"Young," he said. "He's a millionaire and she's about to become the wife of one."

"Lucky girl," she said, then looked around her shop thoughtfully.

He glanced around, too. Everything in her store

seemed designed to appeal to feminine tastes—to women, with perhaps the occasional husband in tow.

He was lost.

Her eyes alighted on something and she took a few steps forward. He followed.

"What about crystal candlestick holders?" she suggested.

The candlestick holders on a nearby shelf were about a foot high and had deep, crisscrossing cuts.

He knew he'd be sending a more expensive gift to Dev and his bride in the future, but he liked the thought of bringing something with him tomorrow, to add to the significance of the day.

Venus looked from him to the candlesticks and back. "Crystal is always appropriate, always timeless, always—"

"Sold," he said. "I'll take them."

She looked surprised but pleased.

He took one of the candlestick holders off the shelf and turned it over. The price was hefty, but he could well afford the cost, especially since the purchase would be worth every penny if it won him points with Venus.

After she took the other holder off the shelf, he handed the one he was holding to her.

As she took it from him, their hands brushed, sending a little electric charge through him—and, if he wasn't mistaken, judging by her sudden tension, through her, as well.

The moment was over in the span of a few seconds, however, and she quickly turned away toward the back of the store.

He followed her as she walked to the checkout counter.

"Is there anything else I can show you?" she asked over her shoulder.

Yes, you. He admired the view of her from the back. *Spectacular.* He thought about how she'd fit in his arms.

Aloud, he forced himself to say, "That's it for this time."

There'd be plenty of other occasions over the course of the coming month, if he had anything to say about it.

She went around the counter and he stopped in front of it.

He watched as she pulled the price tag off his purchase and then wrapped both candlestick holders in tissue paper.

The sight of her slim, manicured hands readying his purchase was arousing.

He needed to get a grip, he thought. Or better yet, get laid.

"Are you staying in Tahoe or just passing through?" she asked, interrupting his reverie.

"I'm staying in Hunter's Landing for a few weeks," he responded. Referring to his stay in terms of mere *weeks* somehow made the upcoming month more palatable.

"Oh, really?" She glanced up. "I live near there."

"Hunter's Landing is small and quiet," he said with a grimace.

He figured she probably assumed he was here for a vacation. He was dressed in khakis and a polo shirt for a change. His usual uniform consisted of custom-made suits and power ties.

"I like small and quiet," she responded.

Small. Quiet. She didn't sounded like a party animal, he thought. Maybe she was in a relationship and felt little need for the local bar scene.

She wore no ring, but there could be a boyfriend in the picture. Or, more likely, *boyfriends,* he amended, figuring men panted after Venus.

"Since I'm not familiar with Hunter's Landing," he said, "maybe you can tell me where I can find a good meal."

He was stretching the truth, since he'd grown up literally next door, on his family's estate in Clayburn, and he'd been to Tahoe on many occasions.

But not in recent memory. Lately he'd been bent on revenge, and Tahoe was too much of a local playground for Webb Sperling and his ilk.

On top of it all, the caretaker of the lodge had left the refrigerator there stocked with gourmet food, but Venus didn't have to know that.

She seemed to consider him, as if wondering whether he was putting the moves on her.

Desire washed over him in a wave.

Her top was a typical V-neck but, since her breasts were at least a C cup, almost anything on her would have looked sexy.

He could also see now, with more intimate inspection, that her eyes were amber shot through with green and gold.

Eventually, she said, "There's not much going on in Hunter's Landing."

Now there was an understatement.

"There's the Lakeside Diner," she went on, "and, of course, Clearwater's, which has a deck overlooking the lake."

Oh, yeah. He could picture a little romantic dinner, moonlight glinting off the water, followed by a retreat to the lodge. They'd sip some red wine and maybe take a dip in the hot tub, all the while listening to some mellow jazz. Then he'd peel off her clothes and they'd make love in the oversized master suite.

He tried to unfog his brain as she deposited his purchase in a ridiculous yellow bag displaying the Distressed Success name.

"Clearwater's sounds great…" He paused. "I didn't get your name."

"Kelly."

"Kelly." He held out his hand. "Ryan."

She shook his hand and he felt long, elegant fingers, her delicate palm tapering to a slim wrist.

The moment seemed to draw itself out, until she finally withdrew her hand.

"How would you like to pay for your purchase?" she asked.

As he pulled out his wallet, he wondered whether he'd only imagined that her voice had sounded husky. "AmEx okay?"

She smiled. "Of course."

Anything to make the customer happy, he thought. She was the consummate saleswoman and, having grown up as an heir to the Sperling department stores fortune, he knew something about the art form.

He handed her the credit card. "I'd enjoy having some company at Clearwater's." He'd eaten alone way too often lately. "Are you available for dinner tomorrow night, Kelly—? I didn't get your last name."

Tomorrow was Saturday. *Smooth, smooth.*

"It's Hartley," she said easily.

As she glanced down at the credit card he'd handed her, a weird feeling washed over him.

One of Webb Sperling's many mistresses had been named Hartley, and the woman had had a daughter with the name Kelly.

Kelly's smile died at the same time as the one on his lips froze. He watched as her eyes widened and her lips parted.

Damn it.

Recognition seemed to slam into her at the same time it did into him.

He cursed under his breath. To think, he'd almost got taken in by a bimbo, just like his father. *Almost,* though. Fortunately, he didn't have Webb Sperling's susceptibility to trashy women.

He'd worked hard his whole life to avoid comparisons to his father. Luckily, his looks came from his mother—a debutante from a rich family—who'd been a dark-haired beauty, right up until cancer had claimed her, just as it had his friend Hunter.

Beautiful, of course, was just the way Webb Sperling liked them, he thought cynically, staring now at Kelly.

Beautiful and money hungry. No wonder she'd thought Dev's bride was lucky to have landed a millionaire.

She'd chosen well for the location of her store. Tahoe catered to people with money to burn. Just like her mother, she seemed to have an unerring sense of where to find easy money.

If he had a say, though, Venus would be ruined.

"You're Webb Sperling's son," she said.

"And you're Brenda Hartley's daughter," he responded grimly.

How could she not have recognized him?

Easily, Kelly answered herself. She hadn't seen him in more than a decade, since before she'd left

Clayburn, and he'd become something of a press-dodging millionaire. From time to time, she'd read newspaper articles about his business dealings, but that was about it.

Of course, the intervening years had wrought a transformation in him.

Any hint of teenage lankiness was gone, replaced by lean muscle and the good looks of a movie star. Though she was tall and wearing heels, he easily topped her. And unlike Webb Sperling—who was blue-eyed and fair, though his hair had been turning white for years—Ryan was dark. With chocolate-brown eyes and dark hair, he had a face that was all Roman god.

She'd felt her breath leave her body when he'd walked in the door. When she'd been a teenager, she'd also found him overwhelming, though then she'd merely stolen glances of him from a distance.

Back then, she'd have been tongue-tied and dumb-struck if Ryan Sperling had deigned to speak to her. He was only two years older, but his wealth and re-bellious bad-boy attitude had made him seem far removed from her in worldliness and sophistication.

She'd never had an actual crush on him—she'd been far too practical for that—but she'd been able to appreciate his seductive appeal.

Rumor around town had been that Ryan was aware of his father's affairs and resented him for it. Ryan's mother had fallen ill and died around the time that Webb Sperling had been involved with Brenda Hartley, and, soon after, Ryan had departed for college, not to be seen around Clayburn again.

She watched now as Ryan's lips curled. "Well, if this isn't a strange coincidence."

The look on his face hardened. Clearly, he was aware of the history their parents shared.

"Or maybe not so strange," he drawled.

She tensed. "How so?"

He rubbed his jaw. "I'm finding it hard to believe you didn't recognize who I was the minute I came into your store."

Her eyebrows knitted. "And why would I pretend not to know you?"

He shrugged. "Perhaps you were trying to impress me without seeming to, hoping I'd run back to tell the Sperlings what a tremendous little entrepreneur you are."

Her eyes widened. So he knew about her negotiations with Webb Sperling to get her designs into Sperling department stores.

She felt herself flush and an uncomfortable feeling swept over her. She was still uneasy about accepting a favor from her mother's loathsome former lover, even if she was desperate to realize her dreams for Distressed Success.

His lips curved without humor. "Sort of like a chef pretending not to know when a food critic is in the restaurant." He looked around her shop, his expression disdainful. "Except you calculated wrong, because I'm not in Webb Sperling's orbit these days."

So, she thought, Ryan's relationship with his father hadn't improved over the years. The rebellious teenager had transformed into an estranged son.

Aloud, she countered, "If that's the case, then how could you know about any discussions I *might* have had with Sperling, Inc.?"

Her negotiations with Sperling were still in their early stages. She had yet to see a contract, in fact.

"I have my sources."

She raised an eyebrow. The idea of Ryan engaged in corporate espionage struck her as funny, even under the circumstances. "A spy?"

"It's not spying when it's all in the family," he asserted.

"And you all get along so well," she shot back.

She knew the company that owned Sperling department stores was completely family owned, its shares divided among various Sperling extended family members.

"I'm not like my sordid parent," he said bitingly, looking her up and down. "That's more than I can say for you."

She bristled.

"On second thought, I should have recognized you. The similarity to your mother can't be missed."

She felt heat rise to her face again as her temper

ignited. She's spent years making sure she *didn't* become her mother. She'd worked hard to get where she was—and, unlike *some people,* she hadn't had the benefit of family money to back her up.

She couldn't do anything about the curvaceous figure and dark coppery red hair that she had in common with the loose-living, fun-loving Brenda Hartley. But these days, people around Tahoe knew her as the owner of a successful small business and as a respectable member of the community. And that's just how she liked it.

"Let me show you the door," she managed, gritting her teeth.

He tossed some bills on the counter, much more than the crystal candlestick holders were worth. "Consider this my contribution to the cause."

Two

"Phew! Who was that?" Erica said as she glanced back toward Distressed Success's front door, where she had just entered and Ryan had just departed. "Looked like Mr. Tall, Dark and Dangerous."

"Mr. Tall, Dark and Irritating is more like it," Kelly responded, wrinkling her nose. She was still steaming over Ryan's attitude.

Kelly had hired Erica, a cute blonde and married mother of two, to help her out in the shop part-time, and her assistant was just showing up for the day.

As Erica continued toward her, she looked down

at the bills scattered on the counter. "Well, it seems as if he liked what he saw."

"Yes," she agreed acerbically, "until he realized *whom* he was seeing. *That* was Ryan Sperling."

Erica's eyes widened.

"Yep," she said in confirmation, "Webb Sperling's son."

She glanced down at the counter. Ryan had left double what the candlestick holders had cost.

Damn Ryan Sperling, she thought. He made her feel unclean accepting his money, just as she felt unclean doing business with Webb Sperling.

"It's too bad he turned out to be someone you'd never want to get involved with," Erica responded. "He's the hottest guy to walk in here in months."

"I hadn't noticed." *Liar, liar.*

"What's he doing in Tahoe?" asked Erica, picking up the scattered bills.

She shrugged. "Taking a vacation, I assume. And with any luck, I won't be running into him again."

She filled Erica in on the encounter with Ryan.

Since being hired to work at Distressed Success three years ago, Erica had become her close friend. Though Kelly was cautious about what she told people regarding her past, she'd confided in Erica about her childhood in Clayburn and her mother's affair with Webb Sperling. More recently, Erica was aware of her negotiations with Sperling, Inc. and how they'd come about.

"From what you've told me," Erica said finally, "he wasn't too happy about your doing business with Webb Sperling."

"Well, there's nothing he can do about it."

Yet, despite how adamant she sounded, she found herself shaking off a feeling of unease.

"Still, maybe it's best if you got this contract with Webb finalized, sooner rather than later," Erica observed.

I couldn't agree more, Kelly thought.

"I'm going to get back to opening those boxes of merchandise that arrived yesterday," Erica announced.

"Thanks."

After Erica had headed back to the stockroom, Kelly found herself left alone with thoughts that she couldn't push away.

The encounter with Ryan Sperling had shaken her up more than she cared to admit to Erica. Ryan exuded power, even a little ruthlessness, and he made her nervous on every level.

By Ryan's own admission, however, he and his father were estranged, so there was little he could do to meddle in her negotiations with Sperling, Inc. Or was there?

She knew from press reports that Ryan had made a fortune gobbling up cable companies. She'd also read he'd inherited from his paternal grandfather a small minority of shares in the family business, but other than that, he had nothing to do with the Sperling retail chain.

On the other hand, Ryan seemed as if he'd be all too eager to upend his father's best-laid plans, particularly when they had anything to do with his former mistress.

Somehow, Ryan had known about her attempt to get her goods into Sperling stores and he'd seemed none too pleased at the prospect.

Kelly shook her head. Of course, she wouldn't be in this predicament if she hadn't said more than she wanted to her mother.

She still rued the day she'd confided in Brenda that she hoped to find a national retailer to carry designs under the Distressed Success name.

The last time her mother had breezed through Tahoe, Brenda had been short on cash *again* and looking for "a small loan," and, as usual, Kelly had offered up some money, knowing she'd never be repaid.

Brenda had taken the opportunity to look around Distressed Success and comment on the latest inventory.

"These jewelry boxes are gorgeous, tootsie," Brenda had said, holding an embroidered silk and stone-encrusted case.

"Thanks," she'd said, walking over. "I hired a manufacturer to produce samples from some designs I sketched. I'm selling some of the samples in the store, but I'm hoping to find an outside vendor for them, too."

She hoped if the samples sold well in Distressed Success, she'd have an easier time getting a big chain to carry them. Her dream wasn't to carry other designers' goods in her boutique, but to build up Distressed Success into a national, even international, brand using her own designs.

Brenda perked up. "A vendor?"

Her mother turned the jewelry box around in her hands, inspecting it. Her nails were long, manicured and fire-engine red, a color that matched her lips.

Not for the first time, Kelly wished her mother would tone it down. Brenda's makeup was perfect for television or for the Las Vegas showgirl she'd once been, but in the harsh light of day, it just looked garish.

Then again, Kelly reflected, since her mother's life often resembled a soap opera, the makeup wasn't completely inappropriate. Brenda continued to live in the fast lane, her devil-may-care attitude still going strong in her fifties.

Kelly sighed. As a teenager, she'd been embarrassed by her mother's loose living. Her mother had drunk, smoked and partied hard. And now it appeared some things were destined never to change.

"I'm looking to partner with a national chain," she said in response to her mother's inquiring look, "but there's a lot of competition for shelf space, especially in the more prestigious retailers."

She could only fantasize about getting her designs in Neiman Marcus or—

"What about Sperling?" Brenda said, her eyes sharpening.

For a moment, Kelly thought she'd spoken out loud, but then she realized Brenda was giving voice to what she herself had been thinking.

"I could contact Webb and—"

"No," she said emphatically. It would be a bad idea for either of them to let Webb Sperling back into their lives.

"It's settled," Brenda said animatedly, putting down the jewelry box. "I'll just give Webb a call and—"

"No."

But Brenda was already caught up in another one of her schemes. "Of course, he's still married to that cheap slut Roxanne—" Brenda's mouth curved in a hard smile "—but Webb and I keep in touch."

Kelly resisted rolling her eyes. As far as Kelly knew, Brenda and Webb hadn't been lovers in years. But one could never tell with those two, particularly since Webb was a known adulterer and Brenda had never looked a gift horse in the mouth.

Kelly mentally winced at the thought of her mother approaching Webb for a favor, then winced again as another, more ominous thought occurred and she wondered whether Brenda had *already* been approaching Webb from time to time over the years for "a small loan."

In the end, she'd convinced Brenda to back off the idea of contacting Webb Sperling—or rather, she thought she had.

Two weeks later, however, the phone call had come. Webb's tone had been too hearty, his attitude a tad oily.

She hadn't had the willpower to resist what was being dangled in front of her, particularly since all her dreams for Distressed Success were bound up in it.

Now, though, she'd unexpectedly come face-to-face with the avenging angel—someone who despised Webb Sperling and everything associated with him. *His son.*

Still, Ryan's attitude riled her. He had some nerve to judge her.

When they'd both been teenagers in Clayburn, he'd been the scion of the richest family in town and she'd been the daughter of the local sexpot and living in a run-down house in the cheapest part of town. Sure, her mother had had an affair with Ryan's father, but only because the senior Sperling liked his women brassy and trashy.

Her world and Ryan's couldn't have been more different—growing up, the only times she'd see him was when she'd occasionally spot him around town. He'd attended exclusive private schools, while she'd been a student at the local high school.

And though he'd had a reputation for hell-

ANNA DePALO   33

raising, his rebelliousness hadn't prevented him from getting into Harvard. She, in contrast, had worked her way through two years of community college to earn a degree in small-business administration and management.

The same will to succeed, however, now made her pick up the phone sitting on the counter. She needed to put her mind at rest, or try to.

When Webb's secretary picked up, she said, "I'd like to speak with Mr. Sperling, please."

"Who shall I say is calling?"

"Tell him it's Kelly Hartley of Distressed Success."

"Please hold while I see if he's available," the secretary intoned.

After she'd endured an anxious wait of several minutes, Webb came on the line.

She'd been afraid he wouldn't be in since it was already Friday afternoon and her recollection from her days in Clayburn was that Webb liked his golf game.

"Kelly, what can I do for you, sugar?" Webb said heartily.

She hated being called sugar, but it appeared to be Webb's favorite endearment.

"Thank you for taking my call," she began.

"There's no need to be so formal, sugar. After all, we're old friends, aren't we? Next time, you just tell my secretary that it's Kelly calling."

Ignoring the invitation, she went on, "I thought

I'd check to see where matters stood as far as putting
through orders for Distressed Success's designs."

Webb sighed. "You have to be patient, sugar. I've
passed along your information to the right people."

"Yes, but—"

"You could say we have a sort of committee
system around here for bringing in a new vendor,"
Webb said jocularly. "Lots of hoops to jump through."

She'd heard the speech before, but it had already
been weeks since she'd heard from any of his
people. "I know, but it's been a while since—"

"Listen, sugar, there's a meeting I need to get to.
Say hello to your mama for me, you hear?"

Webb ended the call before she could argue
any further.

Kelly bet his *meeting* was an appointment on the
golf course.

"What's wrong?" Erica asked, walking back
into the room.

"I called Webb Sperling to check on things, and
got nowhere," she replied. "He told me to be patient,
etcetera, etcetera."

"Still thinking about your run-in with Ryan
Sperling?"

"Among other things."

Erica shook her head. "Don't let a man shake you
up. Trust me, it isn't worth it—" she stopped and
grinned "—particularly when you aren't even
sleeping with him."

An image of her and Ryan making love flashed through Kelly's mind, sending a shiver of awareness shooting through her.

Appalled, she tried to banish the image.

She was sick, *sick,* to even be thinking of Ryan that way after he'd basically accused her of being a skank and made it clear what he thought of her business.

The guy was obviously a jerk with tons of baggage—baggage she didn't need. She already had enough luggage herself to ground a 747.

Erica waved a hand in front of her face. "Earth to Kelly. Come in, Kelly."

"Sorry," she responded, focusing on Erica again.

"Was it something I said?" Erica joked. "You know—" Erica looked at her shrewdly "—Ryan may be a jerk, but there's no denying he's a wealthy, good-looking jerk."

"Really?" she asked, injecting her voice with a healthy note of skepticism.

"Mmm-hmm."

"Hey, you're a married mother of two."

"And not dead."

"What would Greg say?" she pressed.

Greg, Erica's husband, was a hulking firefighter.

"Actually," Kelly added, her tone turning thoughtful, "the image of Greg pounding Ryan to a pulp holds some appeal." Until now she hadn't known she possessed a bloodthirsty streak.

"I think it would be an even fight," Erica responded. "Ryan Sperling looked like no pushover."

And that's what she was afraid of, she thought, pushing aside her unease once again.

She forced herself to switch gears. "Good news. How could I have forgotten to mention it when you walked in? I've been officially hired for the decorating job at the lodge."

Erica clapped her hands. "Fantastic!"

Kelly nodded. "I met with Meri again yesterday, briefly toured the rooms of the house that need decorating and signed a contract."

She and Erica had been discussing the lodge ever since the caretaker for the mysterious home—a woman named Meri—had walked into Distressed Success, taken a look around and talked to them about decorating some empty bedrooms.

Meri, a good-looking woman with an incisive mind, had been short on details about the lodge. It wasn't until Kelly had met with her on Erica's day off yesterday that she'd gotten any real particulars about the house—luxurious even by Tahoe standards—about which speculation had been rife among the locals during the nearly twelve months it had taken to build it.

"For some reason the lodge is now being transformed into a restorative place for cancer patients and survivors," she said to Erica.

Erica raised her eyebrows. "The plot thickens."

"Officially," she went on, "Distressed Success has been hired by the Hunter Palmer Foundation, which got the original building permits. The home has never been fully furnished, and now that it's going to be a restorative place, they need to complete the decor ASAP."

Erica cocked her head. "Why aren't they going with the original decorator?"

"The original firm is too busy right now to take on any more business." And happily, *she'd* turned out to be the beneficiary of the scheduling difficulty. "Meri wants this project completed in the next few weeks in order to cause as little inconvenience as possible to any future occupants."

Erica's brow furrowed. "Lots of work for you."

Kelly gave her a game smile. "No sacrifice is too great where Distressed Success is involved."

"You've got to lighten up," Erica grumbled.

"I will. *After* I put the *success* in Distressed Success. I want the Distressed Success name in every bathroom, every bedroom, every living room—"

Erica rolled her eyes. "Good grief. I'm working for a megalomaniac."

Kelly stopped and grinned. She'd almost forgotten how badly her day had started. Almost. "Sorry. I got carried away."

"So when do you start?"

"I'm visiting the lodge on Sunday, since the shop is closed then. Meri gave me the key to the front door yesterday. She shuttles back and forth to Los Angeles, and she wanted to make sure I'd have easy access. The house will have an occupant for the coming month, but he's been told about the decorating project."

Meri had been tight-lipped about who had been using the lodge, but rumor among the locals was that a man had stayed there in March, another in April and a third in May. Kelly assumed they'd been vacationers who'd paid to rent the place, and that the man due to check in this weekend was there for a similar stay.

"Do you need me to come along?" Erica asked.

Kelly shook her head. "Sunday is your time with the kids. Meri hired Distressed Success because we're local and this project needs to be done fast. Now that I've seen the lodge, I think I know what she's looking for."

Sunday couldn't come too soon for her. She was relishing diving into a new project. Just let Ryan Sperling try to stomp on her dreams!

Sunday morning, Kelly got up early and drove over to the lodge.

Although decorating the house would eat into her leisure time, she was eager to have another venue to showcase her designs. She had no illusions about how competitive the home-decor market was and she'd already spent years improving her designs.

As she got out of her car, she looked up at the famed log-and-stone house. At 9000 square feet, with a soaring sloped roof suspended on thick log columns, the home would surely satisfy any millionaire's luxury tastes. Multistoried, with covered decks on the main level, the house sloped down to the water on one side and had a spectacular view of Lake Tahoe.

Her feet crunched on the ground in front of her as she crossed to the house and traversed the porte cochere to the front entrance.

It didn't look as if anyone was at home, but she rang the doorbell a few times anyway. She waited a moment and, when she received no response, she let herself in with the key Meri had given her.

Stepping into the great room, she caught her breath, impressed all over again. A massive fireplace dominated one wall and large armchairs stood before it. An immense metal chandelier was suspended from the vaulted ceiling, which was braced with wood beams. Windows and French doors afforded a wonderful view of the lake, which glittered under the gaze of the morning sun, the sunlight catching and sparkling like so many diamonds scattered across the waves.

She turned around and looked back at the grand staircase that led to the upper level, where Meri had told her the master suite and guest bedrooms were located. Only two of these rooms had been furnished so far.

Hearing a click, she whirled around, realizing she was no longer alone.

"What the hell—"

Ryan Sperling, naked except for a gray towel riding low on his hips, stood silhouetted by the French doors leading to the deck outside. Droplets of water clung to his torso. Ryan's expression was thunderous, and Kelly sucked in a breath.

She drank in the sight of his smooth, muscled chest, flat stomach and hair-roughened legs, which ended at feet planted firmly on the plush carpeting.

She knew from her first tour with Meri that there was a hot tub on the deck. He must have been soaking in it.

"What the hell are you doing here?"

"I—" Shock rendered her momentarily speechless.

"If this is some desperate attempt to try to persuade me that Sperling department stores should be doing business with you," Ryan sneered, "forget it."

She couldn't believe his ego. He'd already informed her that he didn't have anything to do with Webb these days. Did he really think she'd seek him out as a supplicant for any leverage he *could* provide as far as getting her products into Sperling department stores? *Apparently so.*

Ryan's expression darkened even more. "If this is some sort of entrapment scheme, I've got some of the best lawyers in the country on retainer."

Her temper rose. "Not to worry. Entrapping *you* is the last thing on my mind."

He scowled. "How did you track me down?"

"Easy," she retorted, "I just followed the trail of fawning women."

He smiled mirthlessly. "I've got news for you. Women don't faint for me, they just press their phone numbers into my hand. But this is the first time one's gotten into my house unannounced."

"You'll have a hard time tossing me out," she said, letting a note of satisfaction creep into her voice.

"Why's that?"

"I'm the newly hired decorator."

Three

Ryan figured if he kept talking, he wouldn't get turned on.

Little Miss Sweet and Tart was the last woman he'd expected to discover inside the house, even if he'd had one heck of an erotic dream about her last night. In fact, for a second, when he'd first seen her, he figured he must *still* be dreaming.

He'd been ticked off this morning when he'd realized whom he'd been fantasizing about and that, combined with his current effort to hold those memories at bay, made him brusque.

"Meri said a decorator would be coming by," he

said icily, "but she also said whoever it was would ring the doorbell if she did."

"I *did* ring the doorbell," Kelly said defensively, "but I got no response."

"I was in the hot tub," he snarled, "and I didn't hear you. Then when I did, it took me a minute to get inside to answer the door."

"Clearly."

Great, Ryan thought. It was the first time he'd had a chance to relax in a hot tub since he didn't know when, and now he had to deal with *her.*

It didn't help she was wearing some ridiculous getup that nevertheless managed to be provocative. She had on a white crewneck T-shirt, a long, high-waisted black skirt and black suspenders. The outfit was finished off with midcalf-length black leggings and black pumps.

Her generous breasts were framed by the high waist of the skirt and by the black suspenders. Damn.

"I rang three times," she said.

"I heard only two."

Her chin came up. "Are you suggesting I'm a liar?"

He smiled mirthlessly. "The apple usually doesn't fall far from the tree."

"Same thing goes." She craned her neck. "Anyone out there with you?"

He frowned. *"No."*

She stopped trying to see outside and gave him a cool look. "Well, I'm surprised."

She went beyond irritating, he decided. And what's more, if she was the decorator, then she'd be hanging around the entire time he was here. The realization came as a blow.

"I didn't see a car," she said.

"It's in the garage."

"Oh."

He raked his hand through his hair. "How long is this damn decorating job supposed to last?"

Her lips tightened. "For several weeks, at least. And please try not to refer to it as 'this damn' anything. Some of us have to work or starve."

"Or depend on the generosity of our *friends,*" he sneered.

He figured Brenda Hartley's daughter could spot a sugar daddy as well as, if not better than, her mother. The two certainly looked alike. The pair shared the same voluptuous figure and dark-red hair—and the same siren voice calling men to their doom.

"Let's keep family out of this," she snapped.

"Can't," he responded. "You're trying to shake some more fruit from that tree."

"It's a business deal!"

"Nothing for Webb Sperling is merely business when an attractive woman is involved."

Her mouth fell open. "Are you suggesting I'm *putting out?*"

He raised his eyebrows and she sucked in an outraged breath.

"I don't put out for anyone," she bit out. "Besides, if the newspapers are to be believed, you're just one of many family members who owns a minority interest in Sperling, Inc., so there's not much you can do about my contract with Sperling stores."

"It's not a contract yet, *sugar.*"

Despite her bravado, he sensed her worry he might be able to do something to cause her deal with Webb Sperling to fall through. The hardened business executive in him knew better than to tip his hand, however.

"Look," she said, "I don't like this arrangement any more than you do. Let's just agree to stay out of each other's way. Next time, I'll ring the doorbell until someone responds or call in advance or whatever."

"Nice to hear, but there won't be a next time." He picked up the cordless phone sitting nearby. "I'm calling the caretaker and getting this project postponed or, better yet, cancelled."

The longer he stood in front of her nearly naked, the harder it was to keep thoughts of sex at bay, which fueled his ire, both at her and at himself.

"You wouldn't dare," she said, hurrying forward.

She stopped an arm's length away, visibly fuming as he dialed the cell number Meri had given him.

When Meri picked up after a couple of rings, Ryan spelled out the problem, his eyes on Kelly.

"But I don't understand," Meri said. "I explained

the decorating project to you previously by phone, and you had no problem with it."

"That was before I knew who you'd hired. Ms. Hartley and I have—" how the hell was he supposed to describe it? "—a history. Or rather, *we* don't, but a couple of family members do."

He had no idea why he was protecting the old man by not bringing his name directly into it. The bastard deserved to have his dirty laundry aired.

"Just think of us as friends of the bride and groom, respectively, after there's been a divorce," he told Meri smoothly, regaining some of his cool. "We're on two different sides of the fence."

The caretaker sighed. "Unfortunately, it's out of my hands. Ms. Hartley's been hired by the Hunter Palmer Foundation. The timeline for getting this decorating job done has been spelled out because we wanted to inconvenience the guests as little as possible. By the time you get all this sorted out with the lawyers for the Foundation, your stay will be over. I'm sorry."

Damn it. Into the phone, he said curtly, "Understood."

When he hung up, Kelly asked apprehensively, "Well?"

He contemplated her for a moment. "You're here for the duration—"

She looked relieved.

"—just make sure to stay out of my way. I want

you to let me know when you're showing up—and ring the damn doorbell!"

With those words, he stomped out of the room and up the staircase to the master suite so he could get some clothes on.

His stay in Tahoe was getting off to a rotten start. First, running into Kelly Hartley, and now finding out she'd be wandering around the lodge for the month.

And attending a wedding yesterday hadn't helped.

Having grown up observing his parents' bad marriage, Ryan had never been one for wedding celebrations. Still, he hadn't been able to say no when Dev had asked him to act as his best man. He knew he would have to go to Tahoe anyway to begin his month-long stay at the lodge.

Though even a harsh cynic about happily-ever-after like himself had to admit that Nicole and Dev were well matched, yesterday's wedding was about as close as he ever wanted to come to the altar.

As he made his way down the upstairs hallway, he glanced at a framed photo of Hunter that hung on the wall.

Damn Hunter. Why couldn't his old buddy have just given a big pile of cash to charity and been done with it? Why rope all his old college friends into this ridiculous lodge-sitting relay?

It didn't make sense.

Still, he'd agreed to come to the lodge, willing

to trust that his fraternity buddy had had his reasons. Hunter had in many ways been the deepest thinker in their group.

And the fact that honoring Hunter's will would benefit cancer patients and survivors had been an added incentive. Ryan had been a generous contributor to various charities to fight cancer his whole adult life.

On top of it all, because of his own mother's untimely death from breast cancer when he'd been seventeen, he was a sucker for honoring an old friend's dying wish.

Kelly watched Ryan leave.

Jerk.

Then a sinking feeling settled in her stomach.

She couldn't believe she had to decorate while he was staying here!

She'd been so full of enthusiasm for this project. Now her excitement lay like broken china on the polished wood floor.

And yet, she couldn't forget her initial reaction when he'd walked through the French doors wearing only a towel. Before he'd opened his mouth, heat had shimmered through her and she'd felt the instinctive primal pull of woman to man.

Ryan's chest had been dappled plains, his biceps pronounced and his legs all corded muscle—as if he worked out but wasn't obsessive about it.

There hadn't been an inch of excess on him.
Well, except for, perhaps, *under* the white towel
riding low on his hips and serving as a startling
contrast to the warm tone of his skin.

She heated at the thought, then stopped short.

She had to remember who Ryan was and who
she was.

She could *not* be attracted to Ryan Sperling.

She wasn't like her mother. She wasn't looking
for a quick roll in the sack with a rich guy who'd
throw a few trinkets her way and then toss her aside
without a second glance. She'd built her life refusing
to be that stupid, that careless…*that promiscuous*.

And *even* if she were to be, it would be unwise
for her to get involved with Ryan Sperling, the son
of her mother's former lover and a man who clearly
disdained her.

She hated Ryan's contemptuous attitude.

What had he said? *The apple doesn't fall far
from the tree.*

He knew nothing about her. Nothing about how
hard she'd worked and how far she'd come.

And anyway, if she was mired in mud, so was he.
He was the son of a consummate adulterer.

Added to that, she'd caught the momentary flare
of attraction in his eyes when he'd spotted her today.
Even knowing who she was, he hadn't been able to
contain it.

Her lips curved without humor. Ryan Sperling

was attracted to her, as much as he might hate the fact. Her feminine intuition told her so.

With that thought, she headed toward the unfinished bedrooms. She spent the next half hour measuring the rooms and their respective bathrooms.

She already had some idea of the pieces she'd use to furnish the rooms, but she needed to make sure they'd all fit. She hadn't had time to take measurements on her cursory walk-through with Meri.

When she was done measuring, she stood in the middle of the last room, contemplating.

She knew she'd use Woolrich wool plaid for the curtains and some of the upholstery, accenting and contrasting with some flower and solid prints. She also needed an accent piece or two and had already thought of a deep red leather chair for this particular room.

The house, with its polished wood walls and multiple fireplaces, needed warm tones. Big, comfy furniture would add the finishing touch to its inviting feel.

Her planned theme would fit with the decor in the other rooms of the house, as well as be in keeping with local tastes. Though it wasn't the style she favored for Distressed Success, which had a more feminine appeal, it wasn't a big leap for her creatively, either. She'd lived in Tahoe for several years and become familiar with the local styles.

When her cell phone rang she responded absently. "Hello?"

"Hey," Erica said. "Just wanted to touch base. How are you doing?"

"You'll never believe who's staying here," Kelly responded, her voice lowering. The walls were thick, but she didn't want to risk Ryan overhearing her conversation.

"Don't keep me in suspense," Erica said with a laugh. "I have two kids at home. I may not live to see tomorrow."

"Ryan Sperling."

"What?"

"Under the circumstances, I think I can claim the shorter life expectancy," she said with morbid humor. "It's going to kill me to work here with him around."

Ryan had loved Hunter like a brother, but that didn't prevent him from cursing his old friend over the next few days.

He was holed up in the master suite, trying without success to ignore the noises coming from other parts of the house.

If Kelly hadn't been here, he would have been talking to his longtime lawyer, Dan Etherington, from the great room downstairs. Or while lounging on the outdoor deck. Or while ensconced in the office loft.

Instead, he was organizing a clandestine operation out of his temporary bedroom.

"Will he sell?" he said into the phone.

His father's cousin Oliver had been the last hold-out among the family members he'd approached with an offer to buy their shares in Sperling retail stores for an outlandish amount.

The others had gone quietly, tempted by a payday that would permit them to live out their days on a perpetual holiday in Saint-Tropez. They knew Webb Sperling's inflated ego would never permit him to take the family company public, allowing them to each make real money from the sale of their ownership stakes. A sale to another family member—even an estranged black sheep such as Ryan— was the only type of transfer that wasn't restricted by the bylaws of the corporation.

"He's finally been persuaded, it seems," Dan replied.

Ryan laughed mirthlessly. "Must be my charm."

Oliver had lived a life devoted to fast cars, fast women and fast cash for all of his fifty-nine years. The only thing that set him apart from Webb Sperling was the lack of a managerial position in the family company.

"The charm of your greenbacks is more like it," Dan responded drily.

With the acquisition of Oliver's share in Sperling department stores, Ryan would have finally and quietly acquired enough shares for a controlling interest.

Enough shares, he thought with a rush of triumph, to oust Webb Sperling.

His hand tightened on the receiver. He could taste victory and the flavor was sweet. Still, years of playing corporate hardball had taught him to rein in his emotions—and not count on anything until he was ready to spring the trap.

Though other family members, aside from Oliver, were already on board, Ryan was waiting to take the final step in purchasing their shares until he could count on Oliver's. He wanted to make sure Webb Sperling remained in the dark until the last possible moment, when he'd be presented with Ryan's ownership as a done deal.

He was also counting on the fact that there was no love lost between Webb and other family members to keep Webb clueless.

"People want to sell while they can," Dan went on. "You're benefiting from the impression among family members that Webb Sperling is content to sit on his laurels and isn't doing much to keep Sperling stores ahead of competitors."

"My father has been mismanaging things since he took the helm of the company a decade ago," Ryan responded. "For things to be different, he'd have had to show a discipline he's never possessed."

Webb Sperling had become CEO and chairman of the board of Sperling department stores upon the untimely death from a heart attack of his older brother—Ryan's uncle—who'd succeeded Ryan's grandfather.

The general impression in the corporate world was that Webb was an absentee CEO and that much of the work and decision making was done by those lower in command.

"Well, you finally hit the magic number for Oliver," Dan noted.

"Everyone's got his price," Ryan said cynically. "Now that Oliver's given us his verbal okay, I want the transfer of shares done ASAP. The last thing I need is for him to change his mind."

"I'm sending the paperwork to his attorney as we speak," Dan replied.

After ending his call with Dan, Ryan glanced around the room.

A noise from downstairs alerted him to the fact that Kelly was still in the house.

Damn it.

He felt trapped. It was a feeling he was unaccustomed to and he didn't like it.

Suddenly a loud thud sounded from another part of the house.

Ryan swore and strode to the door.

Four

Walking through the open doorway of one of the unfurnished bedrooms, Ryan pulled up short at the sight that greeted him.

Kelly sat on the floor surrounded by cardboard boxes, curtain rods, yards of fabric and an old wooden ladder.

She glanced up at him distractedly and he wasn't sure whether to be annoyed or amused. Women never looked through him. He could say without ego that he was a commanding presence.

She, on the other hand, looked young and fresh faced sitting on the floor, her hair pulled back in a ponytail and her face devoid of makeup. She was wearing jeans and a pink T-shirt that she looked like she'd been poured into.

After quelling a rush of lust, he reluctantly realized she wasn't too different from the way she'd been a few years ago. She was young and eager to make her mark on the world, full of bright dreams and hungry to see them to fruition.

He had to remind himself she was also a scheming little hussy, just like her mother.

"I heard a crash," he said.

He didn't want to admit to the alarm he'd felt when he thought she might have been hurt.

"I accidentally backed into a box that I'd left on the ladder." She shrugged. "It won't happen again."

"I'd be grateful for small favors."

Sexual awareness made his tone mocking. She'd been here three days in a row now, and her constant presence was starting to wear on him.

Every time she'd shown up, she'd been in some outfit guaranteed to entice, though never overtly sexual.

On Monday, she'd been wearing a short-sleeved striped shirt that resembled many of the ones *he* owned, except hers had had a bright white collar and cuffs. She'd paired it with midcalf-length black khakis and ballet flats.

On Tuesday, she'd been wearing an outfit he'd been at a loss even to describe. There'd been some sort of white peekaboo peasant blouse, a knee-length skirt, and peep-toe plaid sling backs.

Who the hell wore plaid shoes? he'd thought, right before the effect of her whole outfit had slammed into him like a fist of lust.

He knew she showed up at the lodge before or after her day at Distressed Success and, now that he knew how she dressed for work, he wondered that she didn't get more male customers. *Lots more.*

Today, mercifully, she was dressed a little more normally. Like him, she wore jeans—but that pink top was giving him ideas.

He looked around in a deliberate attempt to cool off. "*You* hauled in this stuff?"

She must have when he'd been on the phone.

"Yes," she replied.

"Tell me you're not planning to do this yourself."

"Have you got a better idea?" she asked, her tone defensive. "I need to stay on schedule with this project, and I need to get things done whenever I can get away from the shop."

"Who's holding down the fort?" he asked curiously.

"Erica, the employee who walked in when you walked out on Friday." She added, rising, "Not that it's any of your business."

"You're right," he agreed. "It's not."

He should leave. Now. There was no room for misplaced gallantry in his life.

"I'm about to hang curtains in here."

Her message couldn't have been more clear. She was waiting for him to leave.

"You're going to kill yourself trying to get this job done while keeping the shop open," he found himself saying.

He was acquainted with eighteen-hour days from his own climb to the top of the corporate world.

"I'll get it done," she said, seeming to want to cut off further discussion.

"I'll give you a hand."

She looked as shocked as he felt over his unintended offer.

After a moment, she said, "You're offering to help me?"

He shrugged. Heck, even *he* wasn't sure what motivated him. "There's not too much else to do while I'm here."

"Aren't you on vacation?"

"A *working* vacation," he replied. "I need to stick close to the phone and computer."

Until I oust Webb Sperling, he added silently.

He needed to be available for any communications from Dan, and though he had capable managers at his company, El Ray Technology, *he* had the final say as founder and CEO.

She folded her arms. "Okay, what do you know about hanging curtains?"

"I did volunteer work on low-income housing in

high school." He shrugged. "I went to a place where character-building activities were big on the agenda."

There hadn't been nearly enough of the character-building stuff going on in the Sperling family. But he'd managed to hammer and paint his way into Harvard.

She dropped her arms. "Why would you want to help me? After all, you'd be helping my business and you've already made it clear what you think of the direction that's heading in."

"Maybe I'm hoping to distract you so you'll forget all about Sperling, Inc.," he said with dry humor.

"I frown on corporate sabotage," she said disapprovingly, and he gave a snort of laughter at the earnest expression on her face.

"Aren't you on vacation, even if it is just a working one?" she persisted.

"Not quite a vacation."

In response to her inquiring look, he asked, "How much do you know about the lodge and why it was built?"

"Almost nothing," she replied. "But there was plenty of speculation among the locals when the house went up, and rumor has it there has been a different man staying here every month since March."

"Nathan Barrister, Luke Barton and Dev Campbell," he said, identifying them. "We were all good buddies and housemates at Harvard. Hunter Palmer was a close mutual friend of ours."

"The guy whose foundation built the lodge," Kelly stated comprehendingly.

"Yeah, he's dead." A wave of nostalgia, then sadness, unexpectedly washed over him. They'd all been young and full of hope back then. Much less cynical and hardened to the world.

"I'm sorry."

He fixed her with a bland look. "It's been ten years. He died of melanoma right before graduation. In his will, he set aside money to have the lodge built. If each of the remaining six of us spends a month here, the property will become a rest and recovery place for cancer patients and survivors."

"And that's where I come in with the decorating job," she finished for him.

He inclined his head, then added drily, "Except where you come in is during my damned month."

For the first time, though, he could see some humor in their situation.

Kelly watched as Ryan held up the curtain rod at the level they'd marked on the wall.

"Okay?" he said.

"Mmm-hmm," she responded. She really needed to get her mind off the way his rear end looked encased in those jeans and the way his green shirt stretched across the expanse of his broad back.

She was reluctantly grateful for the help he'd

offered earlier, but she still didn't completely understand why he'd offered it. Plus, he'd said nothing to indicate his opinion had changed about her negotiations with Webb Sperling.

She just hoped the wheels of the administrative process at Sperling, Inc. moved quickly from here on out.

Ryan turned to look at her, and she started guiltily.

He cocked an eyebrow. "How am I supposed to interpret 'mmm-hmm'?"

"Looks good." *Everything* looked good.

"Great," he said, taking the curtain rod off the wall and stepping off the stepladder.

He set the rod on the floor and looked around. "Now that we have the right height, I'll need a screwdriver to get the rod in place."

"I'm capable of doing it myself."

"Yeah, I know, but humor me. I'd be bored otherwise."

"Wouldn't you be bored if I *didn't* challenge you?" she parried.

His eyes glinted. "With women, it depends on the time and place, but since we *are* in the bedroom, I'd have to concede you're right."

"Sexist pig."

He laughed. "I knew that comment would get a rise out of you."

Despite the tremor that went through her in reaction to his words, she decided to steer the conversation to safer ground, and gestured to a pink case on the floor. "It's in there."

He lowered himself to his haunches and opened the case, then looked up at her. "Tool kit?"

"At least we're getting in the game," she shot back.

She sold the woman-sized tool kits in Distressed Success and used one herself at home.

He flashed a grin. "I'll try to adjust."

She was fairly sure he meant to the tools and not to women being in the game but still, she asked, "Why should a woman have to beg and prod her husband or boyfriend to get some curtains hung?"

"I'm all for female empowerment," he said easily, taking the screwdriver out of the case and straightening.

"And yet, given a say in the matter," she shot back, "you'd pull the plug on Distressed Success in a second."

Any hint of humor disappeared from his face. "That's personal."

"How is what I do different from what you do?" she pressed. "You're an entrepreneur and I'm a boutique owner. We're both trying to grow a business."

"I don't try to fleece people with feminine wiles."

"No, you just twist their arm with your money and power," she retorted.

His expression tightened. "Are you going to try to convince me your deal with Sperling has nothing to do with your being the daughter of my father's former lover?"

She threw up her hands in exasperation.

"Look, we've got different perspectives on this issue and neither of us is going to convince the other."

"Agreed."

She watched as he climbed the wooden ladder and started to put a bracket in place for the curtain rod.

It shouldn't have been so sexy to watch him do a menial task, but it was. He was effectively acting as her handyman and she found it all incredibly arousing, no matter how infuriating she found his opinions.

She *really* needed to put their relationship back on a more professional footing, she thought.

"I need to pay you," she said into the silence.

He glanced at her, amusement stamped on his face once again. "Do you know how much I'm worth? The opportunity cost alone would put me out of your price range."

She flushed, but persisted stubbornly, "Still, I ought to compensate you…"

He turned back to put in another screw. "Okay," he said finally, "but I need a point of reference. How much do you charge for *your* services?"

"You couldn't afford me," she responded automatically.

He gave a bark of laughter and looked at her again. "Okay then, we're even."

On the contrary, she disagreed silently. They were far from *even* and she seemed to be losing ground with every passing second.

"All right, when I say lift, we're going to pick up this mattress and set it down upright on its shorter side at the foot of the bed."

Kelly blew tendrils of hair out of her face.

Ryan Sperling, she'd discovered over the course of the past four days, was a man used to issuing commands.

Still, she knew she ought to be charitable. He'd done physical labor uncomplainingly all week. He'd helped her put up curtains, lay down rugs, move furniture and hang pictures. He hadn't even balked when she'd announced today there was a change of plan and she wanted to put this bed in another room.

She watched now as Ryan planted his hands at his waist. "Let's pay attention."

"Right, sorry." There was no way for him to know what she'd been thinking about, but nevertheless heat rose to her face.

She grasped the handles at the sides of the mattress and watched as Ryan did the same on his end.

"Lift," he ordered.

When they got the mattress upright, he grasped it around its shorter side and maneuvered it to lean against the bedroom wall.

Kelly reflected that though Ryan's help had been invaluable these past few days, it had come at a price: their physical proximity was beginning to wear on her.

Just this morning, she'd been aghast to discover she'd dreamed about him. And it hadn't been a sweet dream, either. *No.* In her dream, he'd come to her, massaged her breasts and looked into her eyes with a look of desire. In her dream, he wasn't Webb Sperling's son and she wasn't Brenda Hartley's daughter.

And somewhat more disturbingly, these past few days she could feel his hot eyes on her when he thought she wasn't looking.

What's more, she'd become quite the expert at surreptitious glances herself.

It was clear, however, that his was an unwilling type of attraction. And she didn't know whether to be flattered or offended because she felt likewise.

Of course, it made no sense for her to be attracted to him. From the day he'd walked into Distressed Success, he'd made it clear he thought she was a slut—a floozy, who, like her mother, was one step away from earning her living in one of Nevada's famous brothels.

Wouldn't Ryan be stunned to learn the truth! she reflected. She only *wished* she was having as much fun as her supposed scarlet reputation warranted.

"Now the box spring," Ryan said, heading back toward the bed.

She sighed. "You're comfortable giving commands."

"Yeah, and having them obeyed," he replied with dry humor.

"It wasn't a compliment."

"I'd rather be respected than liked."

"Why can't you be both? Respected and—"

"—inspiring the warm fuzzies?" he finished for her, then shook his head. "Some of us aren't selling romance for a living."

"Well, I haven't heard that one before," she responded. "This is the first time someone has said Distressed Success is *selling romance.*"

He gave her a droll look. "You should use it as an ad slogan. 'Distressed Success. We sell romance.' You'll have those workaholic guys beating a path to your door. Expand your demographic."

"Helping me again?" she said, matching his flippant tone. "At this rate, I'll be ready for the big time before your month is up."

"High standards I can respect," he responded. "They're what set a good business apart from its competitors."

"That's how I feel," she said in surprise.

"Then you've got a decent shot at making something out of your business." He looked down at the box spring. "Ready?"

A little while later, the bed now set up in the next room, Kelly sat down and flopped back on it.

Frowning, he braced his hands on his waist. "What are you doing?"

"Taking a break," she responded.

She surveyed him. He looked none the worse for this afternoon's exertions. In fact, he might as well have just come in from a stroll.

He looked at his watch. "We've got fifteen minutes before you need to get back to the shop. We can hang those two picture frames you wanted in the bathroom."

"Don't you ever stop?" she asked in exasperation. "Erica accuses me of being all work and no play, but I seem like a slacker next to you."

"Just trying to work off some edginess."

"What are you edgy about?" she asked curiously.

His face shuttered. "Nothing."

It clearly wasn't *nothing*.

"I've been jogging," he elaborated, "but I'm not getting the workout I'm used to back home."

"Let me guess. You normally rise at five in the morning to get on the elliptical trainer."

"And let me guess, *you* don't. Instead, you're having tea out of a mismatched cup and saucer."

She shook her head and smiled. "Tea's at four in the afternoon," she corrected. "Civilized."

Civilized, she thought, was what Ryan barely seemed, despite generations of money and breeding in the Sperling family tree. He emanated raw masculinity and barely leashed power.

He eyed her and she belatedly realized how she must look lying before him. She was wearing a sheer emerald green blouse over a snug-fitting beige tank, and had paired them with pedal pushers.

They didn't like each other, she reminded herself. They had just unexpectedly been thrown together this month, and had reached a de facto truce so they could be civil to each other.

His gaze trailed over her. "Yeah, well, don't worry. You're none the worse for not hitting the gym at five. Everything looks good."

Men, she thought, suddenly indignant. He was willing to look down at her, literally and figuratively, but that didn't prevent him from enjoying the view.

"How can you know me so well and yet think so little of me?" she blurted.

He didn't respond, but the look on his face was one of sexual awareness blended with irritation and it spoke of his inner battle.

All at once, she'd had enough. Enough of his scorn, enough of his disdain, enough of his attitude altogether. She'd spent a lifetime feeling answerable for her mother's actions and she'd had enough.

She patted the bed beside her. "Take a break."

He looked from her to the bed, his eyes narrowing.

She almost smiled, feeling a touch reckless—and strangely empowered.

"No, thanks," he said roughly. "Let's get a move on."

She arched a brow. "Does it bother you if I lie here?"

"In a word, *yes*."

His hand closed around her ankle, and he pulled her toward him.

She gasped and sat up, lowering her feet to the floor as she reached the edge of the bed.

"That's better," he said, his eyes gleaming.

She stood up and watched as his gaze went to the cleavage revealed by her V-neck blouse.

When his gaze finally came back to hers, time seemed to slow.

She searched his face. His expression was forbidding, but desire was nevertheless stamped on every feature. *He wanted to kiss her.*

Her lips parted and she felt a tingling awareness all over.

"You don't even like me," she said.

"Yeah, but right now, it's hard to care," he responded.

"This is a bad idea."

"I've had worse," he muttered.

"You're going to kiss me."

"Are you going to object?" he asked, bending toward her.

Her eyes fluttered closed and she sighed as his lips touched hers. His mouth was warm and soft as it moved over hers, shaping and stroking.

Her arms stole up to his neck and his came around her, so that they fit together snugly.

This, she thought, was what she'd wondered about ever since he'd walked into her shop, but the real thing was even better than she'd imagined.

She opened to him, allowing him to take the kiss deeper.

Within moments, liquid desire pooled between her legs and her breasts grew heavy and sensitive.

Her hand ran through his hair, anchoring him, as the heat they generated took them ever higher.

She moaned and shifted, and it seemed to fuel his response and need.

Abruptly, however, he lifted his head and he pushed her away.

"Damn it," he said harshly, his eyes glittering.

She felt off balance, but his reaction soon sunk in.

"Damn it," he repeated, running a hand through his hair, as if unable to believe his own stupidity. "You're the daughter of my father's former mistress. My father was sleeping with your mother while mine was dying!"

His words stung, dredging up feelings of being cheap and unclean—guilt by association with Brenda Hartley.

Her chin came up. "And that sums it up, doesn't it?"

"Those are the facts that you and I can't change," he countered.

"Except you're attracted despite yourself, aren't you, Ryan?" she tossed out. "And you hate yourself for feeling that way."

She turned then, grabbed her purse and bolted from the room.

When she made it down to the lower level of the house, she could hear Ryan's footsteps upstairs.

"Kelly!"

Without heeding his attempt to catch up with her, she yanked open the lodge's front door and walked rapidly to her car.

Moments later, as she pulled out of the drive with a spray of gravel, she let the humiliation sink in.

She would not be that vulnerable to Ryan Sperling again, she vowed.

She, of all people, should have known better.

Five

That night, Ryan nursed a beer at the bar of the White Fir Tavern. As he took a swig of his drink, he looked around him morosely.

The White Fir was your typical rustic roadside bar, except it claimed to have been in existence since 1930. A steady trickle of upscale tourists through its doors lent it some pretension. The wood surface of the bar was so dark and beer stained, it was practically black. An unused pool table stood to one side, along with a fifties-style jukebox.

The place was about half-full, and between the steady drone of conversation and the wail of Chuck

Berry, the waitstaff could be heard calling out orders to the short-order cook.

Ryan glanced behind him. The short blonde at the middle table looked familiar from the day he'd stomped out of Distressed Success. What had Kelly called her—Erica?

She sat now with a big, equally blond guy. A husband or boyfriend, he figured.

Given the way things had gone with Kelly earlier in the day, he wasn't inclined to introduce himself to one of her friends.

In any case, Erica didn't appear to recognize him. Or if she did, she preferred to keep her distance. Maybe Kelly had already confided in her and Erica was calling him ten kinds of rat under her breath.

He shook his head. If women just got over the loyalty thing, he thought wryly, they could rule the world.

On the other hand, *his* major problem appeared to be a lack of self-discipline. He couldn't believe he'd let loose and kissed her.

He needed to have his head examined—or get laid. The second approach had its appeal, but the only woman he was interested in at the moment was Kelly and going to bed with her would only worsen the problem, not lessen it.

He wished to hell his month at the lodge were over. Of all the places in the world, Hunter would have to have chosen Kelly's backyard to build his damn house, and *he'd* have to have chosen the month when she'd be working there, parading her tempting butt in his face.

He took another swig of his beer. He needed to stay away from her.

No more helping out with her decorating. It had been a mistake from the beginning to offer his assistance. He could see that now.

Too bad the only thing he could still see was the memory of Kelly lying across a bed like the greatest temptation.

"So how's it going over there at the lodge?" Erica asked.

"Fine," Kelly said curtly, setting down a lamp with more force than necessary.

It was Friday morning and they were straightening up inside Distressed Success in anticipation of opening the store at ten.

Erica quirked a brow. "Just 'fine'?"

"He's a pain in the butt," she blurted. There was no need for her to explain who *he* was.

Erica laughed. "I thought he was helping you."

"He is."

Beside her, Erica stopped setting out new inventory and searched her face. "And?"

"Yesterday, he kissed me."

Erica's eyes widened, then she grinned. "I

guess he's taken to heart the saying about loving your enemy."

Kelly arched a brow.

"Keep your friends close and your enemies closer?" Erica asked.

"This situation is *not* funny." She'd been brooding all last night over how she was going to face Ryan again. How was she ever going to be able to work at the lodge anymore?

Erica pretended to consider. "Let's see…wealthy, gorgeous guy puts the moves on you." She nodded knowingly. "Yup, definitely not funny."

"Afterward, he regretted it," she said in a rush, reliving the moment. "He couldn't believe he'd committed the unpardonable sin of being attracted to a Hartley. I guess the parallels to his father and to Webb's affair with Brenda were too much for him."

"Jerk," Erica agreed cheerfully. "I should tell you some of the insensitive things Greg said to me when I first met him."

Kelly frowned. "Are you defending Ryan Sperling?"

"No," Erica responded. "He's an arrogant jerk who deserves to be taken down a peg."

"Exactly."

"Still," Erica said, tilting her head, "you haven't told me how *you* felt when he kissed you."

"I—"

The truth was…the truth was, it had been wonderful. She'd felt dizzy with sensation. Aloud, she said, "Does it matter? It ended badly."

"Repressed sexual desire," Erica responded knowingly. "Ryan slipped the leash yesterday and he's pissed off. Still, it's not good to repress emotion."

Kelly sighed impatiently. Sometimes she forgot that she and Erica had bonded over the fact they were both the children of free spirits. Erica was the youngest child of 1960s flower children who'd spent time in Haight-Ashbury, and she…well, *she* was the daughter of Brenda Hartley.

"Ryan's not repressing anything," Kelly replied. "It was just a kiss. Unplanned and spur-of-the-moment." And out of control. "I've been at the lodge all week and he's helped me out. That's it. In the evenings, he takes himself off to who-knows-where."

"The White Fir Tavern," Erica said.

Kelly looked at her blankly. "What? How do you know that?"

"It's where I meet Greg after work so we can drive home together. Greg and I have seen Ryan eating dinner or having a drink at the bar a couple of nights this week."

So *that* was where Ryan went when he left the lodge alongside her in the evenings. She'd wondered where he was going, even though she'd told herself not to.

"Both times there've been women hitting on him, too," Erica supplied.

She felt a stab of jealousy.

Stop it, stop it, stop it, she told herself.

Still, she steamed over Ryan's double standard. Apparently, he was willing to paint *her* as a wanton hussy while *he* hung out with the swinging singles crowd at the White Fir Tavern.

She, meanwhile, had spent her evenings the way she usually did—quietly at home, *alone.* Often, she was simply trying to catch up on billing and other correspondence for Distressed Success.

Erica shrugged. "You'd think Ryan would expect to see you there, offering lap dances to the male patrons, from the things he's said to you."

"Yes," she mused, "he would, wouldn't he?"

This wasn't the smartest idea she'd ever had, Kelly conceded.

Still, now that she was here, she had no choice but to brazen it out.

Inside the White Fir Tavern, she spotted Erica and Greg sharing a table near the center of the pub.

The second thing she noticed was Ryan, sitting at the bar holding a beer, turned mostly away from her and the entrance.

Kelly noticed Erica's eyes widen when she saw her.

She'd told her assistant to go on home, since she just needed to finish closing up shop for the day. Instead, she'd gone to the back of the store and changed clothes before coming on over to the White Fir Tavern herself.

She knew Erica and Greg would be there, maybe sharing a quick drink or some finger food before heading home to the kids and relieving the babysitter, who happened to be Erica's mother.

Of course, the other person Kelly knew she'd find at the White Fir Tavern was Ryan.

But as she moved toward Erica's table, she refused to look around because she didn't want to lose her nerve.

And judging from the look on Erica's face, Kelly knew exactly how she must appear. Her whole outfit begged for attention, from the bronze halter top to the black skirt and three-inch spike heels.

She got plenty of looks from the male patrons—admiring, appreciative and lustful.

As she approached Erica, Greg turned around, too, and his arrested expression put both courage and fear in Kelly's step, since it was probably a good indication of what Ryan's reaction would be.

"Hi," Kelly said brightly, stopping at their table.

"What are you doing?" Erica asked in a low voice.

"Just what we discussed," she responded. "Living up to what's expected of me."

Greg looked from Kelly to his wife. "Anyone care to fill me in?"

Erica nodded her head toward the bar. "It's about the guy over there who's staying at the lodge this month while Kelly is decorating. Ryan Almighty Sperling. He thinks Kelly is a—" she paused and threw Kelly an apologetic look "—slut. Kelly has taken it into her head to make a point."

Kelly watched as Greg looked up at her. "Well, I'd say she made it, all right." His glance moved beyond her, and his lips twitched. "And to the guy at the bar, too."

"Good," she said emphatically, though she felt the hairs at the back of her neck prick. "I'm going to get myself a drink."

She sauntered to the bar, taking care not to look directly at Ryan, though she could sense the heat of his gaze.

"Jack and diet," she instructed the White Fir Tavern's bartender, a genial-looking man in his sixties.

The bartender's eyes crinkled and he set down a napkin before her. "Coming right up. Lady knows what she wants."

She smiled. "Today I do. Thank you."

"What the hell are you doing here?" Ryan said roughly.

She took her time turning to face him.

His expression was grim as his eyes raked her, pausing at her cleavage, where her breasts threatened to spill from the restraint of her halter top.

"What am *I* doing here?" she challenged. "I thought *you* were the newcomer."

His lips thinned. "You know what I mean."

"I'm acting the way you expect me to," she said with defiance. "Isn't this where you thought I'd be?"

Given his opinion of Hartleys, he should think she'd fit right in here among the women hanging out at the White Fir Tavern—and pawing him, if Erica was to be believed.

The bartender set her drink down before her and she picked it up and took a sip, scanning the room. More than a few men continued to look her way—and enjoy.

Ryan threw some bills down on the counter and said grimly, "I'm settling the tab for both of us."

Kelly threw him a flirtatious look, then turned to walk away.

Without invitation, Ryan followed.

She stopped at her table and gestured at Erica and Greg. "Have you met my friends? Erica and Greg Barnes—" she waved a negligent hand in Ryan's direction "—this is Ryan Sperling."

Erica smiled and Ryan and Greg shook hands.

She and Ryan sat down at the small round table.

Erica turned to Ryan. "So, Kelly mentioned you're staying at the lodge while she's decorating."

"Yes, I am." Ryan shot Kelly a look, but she refused to turn his way. "Just for the month."

"How do you like Tahoe?" Greg asked.

"I haven't been here in several years," Ryan responded, shooting her another look. "It's interesting coming back. Some things have changed and others are really *familiar.*"

While Erica and Greg continued to make desultory conversation with Ryan about the local area, the atmosphere at the table continued to carry an undercurrent of tension.

After some time, a young waitress in a low-cut top came around to take an order of drinks. The waitress smiled invitingly at Ryan, who looked as if he didn't mind the attention, and Kelly thought sourly that bare boobs were apparently acceptable on anyone *not* named Hartley. She put in an order for a green-apple martini—one of Brenda's favorites. After that, she remained determinedly distracted, smiling an invitation at the men who happened to look her way.

Eventually, though, Erica and Greg announced they had to get back to the kids.

When everyone rose from the table, Erica leaned close. "I hope you know what you're doing."

Kelly smiled reassuringly. "I'm having the time of my life, can't you tell?"

With a look of semiserious warning, Erica turned toward the door and Kelly took the opportunity to walk back to the bar and settle herself on a stool, leaving Ryan alone at the table.

Ryan's presence had been keeping men away, she thought irritably, and it was time she did something about it.

After she'd ordered another fabulous martini—

why hadn't she discovered them earlier in her life?—she smiled at the attractive man sitting next to her. She'd noticed he'd looked her way occasionally since he'd walked into the bar fifteen minutes ago, and now she met those looks straight on.

He looked to be around thirty, with sandy-blond hair and blue eyes. If it had been wintertime, she would have said he was a ski bum, drawn to the slopes nearby. Tahoe attracted those with money to burn to its slopes, lake and nearby casinos.

"Buy you a drink?" he offered.

She smiled back. "Thank you." Then she leaned closer, conspiratorially. "You're more likable than the other guy who offered to buy me a drink tonight."

She used the term *offered* loosely. Ryan, in typical high-handed fashion, had announced he was settling the bill and that was that.

The man next to her smiled back. "I noticed you the minute I walked in."

She learned his name was Tate and he was another money-to-burn fun seeker vacationing in Tahoe.

All the while, however, she could feel Ryan's eyes boring into the back of her head.

She took another sip of her drink, her third, and thought she had a nice little buzz going.

She cast a sidelong look at Tate, then one at Ryan, who still sat sullenly, beer in front of him, at the table they'd shared with Erica and Greg.

The contrast between the two men couldn't have been more apparent. One was a blond thrill seeker, the other a dark angel with a mission. And the more she talked and flirted with Tate, the more she thought she preferred the former.

She smiled languidly at her bar buddy. He was a nice man, she decided with a warm rush. He was full of effusive compliments that bolstered her confidence, *unlike* another man she could name.

She leaned in, resting her hand on Tate's arm.

Ryan's jaw hardened.

She was tipsy and getting more inebriated by the minute.

Of course, the smooth-talking charmer Kelly was flirting with was enjoying every second of it. Likely, he was waiting for the moment when she was so far gone he could convince her to head home to bed with him.

On top of it all, the guy had thrown him a couple of amused looks, as if he knew he was an interloper and was enjoying the fact.

Ryan's hand flexed on his drink. He itched to slug Prince Charming.

He knew the type. Growing up under Webb Sperling's roof had taught him to identify it.

He told himself he didn't care, but then Kelly leaned toward the guy, laughing, her eyes too bright, and Ryan downed the last of his drink and rose.

As he walked toward the bar, he told himself he was just irritated *this* was the thanks he got for toiling for her all week.

"Are you here with someone?" Charming said to Kelly, noting his approach.

"No—"

"Yes," Ryan cut in, "she's with me."

Kelly swung around. "No, I'm not." She looked beyond him. "Where are Erica and Greg?"

"They left," he responded flatly.

"Oh, right."

He looked at her closely. She'd clearly passed *tipsy* and was well on her way to *ditsy*.

He turned then and sized up the guy she was with.

There was a reason, he thought, that the initials for Prince Charming were *P.C.* The guy looked as if he never put a foot wrong—as if he knew exactly how to ingratiate himself with women.

"Tate Henderson," the guy said, offering his hand.

"Ryan Sperling," he responded, ignoring the hand.

Tate's face registered surprise. "Ryan Sperling? The guy behind El Ray Technology?"

"None other," he responded curtly.

Tate, however, became more animated. "I've heard of you. You're a legend in the cable world, not to mention a favorite on Wall Street. Those shares you offered—"

Kelly stifled a yawn with her hand.

Ryan glanced at her. He was putting a damper on her tête-à-tête with Tate and she clearly wasn't happy about it.

Ryan didn't mind invoking his wealth and power when it suited his purposes, and *now* definitely suited his purposes.

Ryan signaled the bartender and leaned forward, wedging himself between Tate and Kelly to order another drink, tonic water that he intended to sip while he kept an eye on Kelly's Brenda Hartley impersonation.

Turning back after he'd ordered, he took the opportunity to murmur to Tate, "Sweetness is on her way to Happyland. I'm here to make sure she gets home safely—and alone."

Tate raised his eyebrows. "What's she to you?"

"There's a family connection."

The other man's lips quirked up. "It's always something like that."

Tate downed the rest of his drink, then leaned back to reach into the pocket of his jeans.

"Leave it," Ryan said. "I'll settle the tab."

Tate gave a brief nod of acknowledgement and slid off his bar stool as Ryan stepped back from the bar.

Kelly frowned. "Where are you going?"

"It's been a pleasure, *sweetness,*" Tate responded, tossing an amused look at Ryan.

Kelly's frowned deepened. "You're leaving?"

Tate glanced at Ryan. "I'd ask *him.*"

Ryan and Kelly both watched as Tate moved off toward the door, then Kelly swung to face Ryan.

"You chased him off," she accused.

"No chasing was involved."

"Thanks a lot," she muttered. "It's none of your business."

She took another swallow of her drink, then looked surprised when she came up short.

Ryan watched as she signaled the bartender.

"Don't you think you should go easy?" he asked.

"I'm not talking to you."

He sighed and settled down on the bar stool beside her, opposite the one where Tate had been sitting. Clearly, she wasn't going to make this simple.

"If you're looking for some action, why don't you go after the guy you really want?" he challenged.

She surveyed him. "I don't want you."

He arched a brow. "That wasn't the case when you were moaning in my arms."

Her lips pursed. "Go away."

"Can't. That option isn't available to you."

They sat without talking for close to an hour. She made vain attempts to flirt with other men, but Ryan knew his presence—like a dragon at the gate—would keep them away.

He'd have to put a stop to this at some point soon. She was obviously a drinking lightweight and, despite the sex-on-heels outfit, she seemed un-accustomed to the bar scene.

Finally he watched as she finished her drink and tossed a look his way.

He looked back at her.

"You're cute, you know?" she said, her voice a little slurred.

He arched an eyebrow. "Some have said so."

Now *this* was an interesting turn in the conversation.

She tilted her head and touched his hair. "You've got wonderfully thick, dark hair."

He stiffened at her touch, and want shot through him.

"Such deep, dark eyes." She sighed, then pronounced, "Mysterious."

She looked back at his hair and said sadly, "You'd have *beautiful* hair if you kept it longer than almost military length."

An unbidden smile tugged at his lips. Nobody used a soft, frilly word like *beautiful* for him. And though he knew it was the alcohol talking, he felt his body grow taut in response.

She leaned toward him but, when it seemed as if she was about to lose her balance, his hand shot out to steady her, clamping down on her thigh—and staying there.

They both looked down, then she looked up and met his gaze.

"Nice hands, too," she said huskily.

He could see the lovely rays of golden-brown in her hazel eyes and his hand tightened on her leg.

Then he caught himself. He wasn't here so she could hit on him. He was here so he knew she got home okay.

"Let's go," he said.

She sat back. "Go?" she echoed. "Well, that's direct."

"You're slurring your words." He called over the bartender, then covered their tab plus a hefty tip.

She hopped off the bench, showing off mile-long legs and he sent up a prayer for resistance he didn't have.

Then, because she teetered on her heels, he took her arm. And when that didn't seem to do the trick, he bent in one quick motion and swung her into his arms.

She gasped and he could feel every luscious curve of her pressed into him.

He moved toward the front door, and one of the other patrons opened it for him.

He glanced down at her as he walked over the gravel drive to his car. "You know," he said wryly, "I think I like you better drunk."

"You know, I think I like you better when I'm drunk." She frowned, concentrating. "Wait. Did I say that right?"

He smiled. "It came out okay."

She looked at his car. "A black Mercedes. I

wasn't surprised you drive a Mercedes. You've always had money."

He ignored the comment about money. Dangerous territory, he decided, right before he set her down—against the car, just in case.

He got the front passenger door open. "In you go."

She looked around, perplexed. "Where's *my* car?"

"Doesn't matter. You're in no shape to drive."

"Hmm…I guess I agree?"

Then, because she chose to just stand there and he was getting impatient, he picked her up and put her in the front seat.

He reached across her for the seat belt and strapped her in, all the while brushing against her, picking up her scent and testing his endurance even more.

"What's the perfume you're wearing?" he asked roughly.

She smiled. "Sin."

"Of course."

He closed the passenger door and went around the front of the car.

On the drive over to the lodge, she was chatty. She yawned a few times, too, tiredness winning out over the alcohol.

"You're not as bad as you seem," she observed after an interlude.

Her words came out sleepy, and he glanced at her, taking his eyes off the road for a moment. She was striving to keep her eyes open.

"You're doing a good deed by staying at the lodge. Hunter Palmer was your friend and you'll be helping sick people."

"It's my good deed for the decade," he disavowed. "I'm as low and slimy as you think."

If she was calling even *him* nice, she must really be tired or wasted or both.

Six

When they got to the lodge, Ryan pulled into the garage and got Kelly upstairs to the guest suite next to the master bedroom.

Once there, she sat on the bed and looked around. "This room is so pretty. I hope I can do as good a job with the rooms I'm decorating."

"I'm sure you will," he reassured her.

"Do you think so?" she asked hopefully.

He nodded.

There was not much else he could say. The room they were in looked fine to him. Maybe it was be-cause he came from money and took it all for granted, but he'd never been too interested in the aesthetics of his surroundings.

He regarded Kelly. "Are you okay getting undressed and into bed by yourself?"

She flopped back onto the bed so that she was lying in it. "Of course."

He sighed, then reached out and grasped her hands to pull her back to a sitting position. "Okay, sweetness, let's really get you ready for bed."

With her cooperation, he got her shoes off, tugged off her skirt and breathed a sigh of relief when it turned out she was wearing a strapless bra beneath her halter top.

Undressing her was pure torture. He was just glad she was too tired and inebriated to turn up the heat on him even more.

"I'm just like my mother," she said as he tossed her clothes onto a nearby chair.

He stopped because her comment came out of nowhere. "What?"

She looked forlorn. "I'm being undressed by a man I met in a bar."

He wanted to point out that they'd known each other before tonight and that he had no intention of taking her to bed—he just wanted to put her *in* one.

"No matter how hard I try," she said sorrowfully, "I can never escape my mother's past."

Now *that* he could relate to. Hell, he'd been

trying to escape his legacy for more years than he could count.

Aloud, he said, trying to offer some solace, "You're not the only one."

He pulled back the bedcovers and she slid her legs underneath them. Without delay, he tugged the covers up, hiding her tantalizing body from view.

She sank back against the pillows and closed her eyes, and he expelled a breath.

In a moment, however, her eyes opened again. "You forgot to take off my bra."

He clenched his jaw. "I didn't forget." He mentally ran through explanations. "There are no pajamas here for you to wear, so you'll have to sleep in your bra."

The logic wasn't great, but he hoped in her current foggy state, she'd let it pass.

"Hmm," she said, and in the next second, sat up and reached behind her.

Her luscious breasts sprang free.

He couldn't help himself. He took it all in hungrily.

Her breasts were round and firm and capped with tight, dusky pink nipples.

Kelly dropped the bra to the side and lay back down, pulling up the covers as she did so.

"I've never had a man look at them like that before," she murmured, her eyes drifting closed. "But then, I've never been to bed with a man before, either." After a moment, she added more faintly,

"Well, one guy. Once or twice. But he didn't stay the night."

His mind churned with questions, but her peaceful expression told him she'd fallen asleep.

She had dropped quite a few bombshells on him tonight, but damned if she hadn't left the biggest for last.

Kelly woke with a headache.

She moaned and pressed her head into the pillow.

Some of the events of the night before came back and she reflected that she'd drunk more at the White Fir than she'd ever put back at one go in her life.

Making a note to herself that those apple martinis were potent stuff, she finally opened her eyes and looked around.

It took a moment to register she was in the already-furnished guest suite at the lodge.

Her heart seized and she bolted to a sitting position...then moaned again and cupped her forehead.

Ryan had driven her back to the lodge.

With dread, she peered under the covers, and discovered she was naked except for her panties.

She groaned, remembering how she had bared her breasts to Ryan, and how he had fixed his searing gaze on them.

How was she *ever* going to look him in the eye again? Last night made the kiss they'd shared in one of the lodge's bedrooms seem insignificant in comparison. She had bigger problems to think about now—starting with needing to get to work.

She checked the bedside alarm clock. It was seven. Enough time, she thought with relief, for her to get out of here, home to change and then to work at Distressed Success.

Her mind skittered across the fact that she wasn't sure she remembered *everything* she'd said and done last night. What if she'd forgotten something significant?

She winced, then willed herself out of bed and got in the shower. Fortunately, the adjoining bathroom was stocked with towels and toiletries, and the shower helped clear her head.

Afterward, stepping back into the bedroom, she threw on the previous evening's clothes because she had nothing else to wear. She left her panties off, however, and stuffed them in her purse.

She reflected that she *really* was turning into her mother if she was walking around without underwear.

She shook off the thought as she towel dried her hair. Last night *was* an aberration. She was going to go home and resume life as usual.

But first she had to get out of here without a confrontation with Ryan.

When she was done fixing her hair and straightening up the bedroom, she slung her purse over her shoulder, took a deep breath and headed toward the door.

Outside in the hallway, she found herself tiptoe-ing without meaning to.

She told herself that she didn't want to awaken Ryan if he was still asleep. It was only after seven in the morning. Closer to eight, really, but who was around to quibble with her?

She stole down the stairs, then crept toward the front entrance.

"Good morning."

She jumped and turned.

Ryan stood there, an amused expression on his face. He was holding a cup of coffee, and looked relaxed and showered.

"Er— good morning."

He was dressed in jeans and a gray T-shirt, and looked not only clean, but refreshed. It wasn't fair, she reflected, that he should look so put together, while she felt rumpled and tawdry.

"You weren't leaving without saying goodbye, were you?" Then without waiting for an answer, he added, "Coffee?"

She regarded him suspiciously because he looked to be in a good mood.

He *should* be furious with her. He'd definitely seemed so last night. She had gotten wasted, hit on another guy and given him the cold shoulder. Then he'd had to drive her home.

"Um, thanks," she responded, "but I'd prefer just to head home."

He looked her over. "You're looking good this morning…all things considered."

She wanted to tell him that her outfit felt like dessert: Some things were best indulged in before regrets took hold.

His eyes came back to hers and now she could see the flicker of amusement in their depths. "I guess you didn't have a choice but to jump back into last night's clothes."

She looked down at what she was wearing, trying to brazen it out. "What, this? I find a halter top a freshening change from work clothes, don't you?"

"I wouldn't know," he murmured, then looked at her purse. "I guess the underwear is optional."

She followed his gaze and realized with embarrassment that her panties peeked out of her open bag.

Could life get any more humiliating?

"No underwear," he said wickedly. "Just how I like it."

She flushed. He was enjoying teasing her, and unfortunately she was giving him the reaction he wanted.

He seemed to be *flirting* with her, though *that* didn't make sense.

Last night, she'd proven every preconception he'd had of her and then some. She'd acted like her mother and worse.

"Aren't you angry at me?" she blurted.

He tilted his head. "What for?"

"For last night," she tossed out. "I had too much

to drink and you had to get me—" she almost said home, but caught herself "—back from the bar."

There had been more to last night than merely getting drunk, of course, but she left the rest unsaid.

He shrugged. "We all make mistakes. I may have been too harsh."

"You mean, last night?"

He shook his head. "Since running into you at Distressed Success."

A strange skittishness seized her at his admission, but she attributed it to vestiges of her flirtation with the wild side the evening before.

"How much do you remember about last night?" he asked.

The answer seemed to matter to him. "More or less all of it," she hedged.

"Everything?" he probed.

"Enough to know we *didn't* sleep together!" She was sure she'd remember *that* much.

He looked at her thoughtfully, then seemed to switch gears, lightening up and nodding toward the back of the house.

"C'mon," he said. "I'll fix you a cup of coffee, then drive you."

She sighed. "Okay."

She couldn't protest too much. The way her head felt, coffee sounded wonderful.

As they walked toward the back of the house, he asked, "How were you planning to get back, by the way? Your car's back at the tavern." He smiled briefly. "Or were you planning to strand me by car-jacking my car?"

"I knew there were a couple of mountain bikes in the garage," she responded reluctantly.

He looked at her inquiringly.

"I was planning to bike to the gas station down the road," she elaborated, "and then call a cab service to take me home."

He grinned. "You were going to ride a bike wearing a skirt and no underwear?"

She felt herself blush. "I admit it wasn't one of my better ideas."

Minutes later, they got into his car, coffee in hand, and began the drive over to the tavern.

"What about grabbing some breakfast nearby?" he asked.

"I need to get Distressed Success open by ten." His attitude had changed completely this morning, and she still wasn't sure what to make of it.

He glanced at her. "You're the boss. Give yourself permission to show up late."

She cupped her forehead and joked weakly, "I think my interlude of acting irresponsibly ended last night."

"Coffee, and lots of it," he advised, then added, "What about dinner tonight then? You mentioned Clearwater's once and I haven't tried it."

She hesitated. "Thanks, but—"

"—you want to thank me for putting you to bed last night?"

She couldn't argue there. "All right," she said, giving in.

"I'll pick you up. Seven, okay?"

"Perfect."

Less than two hours later, Kelly arrived at Distressed Success just on time. After Ryan had driven her back to the White Fir Tavern, she'd driven home, changed and made her way to the shop.

She watched as Erica pulled up in her car just as she got the front door open.

"Hi," Erica said as she came in moments later. "You're right on time."

"You sound surprised," Kelly responded, flicking on some lights.

Erica gave her a look of open curiosity. "Well, I admit to wondering how last night went…."

"You mean, my moment of glory as the red-haired sex goddess?"

Erica grinned. "Even Greg was surprised, and, let me tell you, after two kids and twenty years in the fire department, it takes a lot to shock that man."

"I got completely and utterly inebriated."

Erica's eyes widened. "Drunk?"

"I was a drinking virgin until last night," she confirmed grimly, putting down her purse and taking off her jacket.

Erica looked at her closely. "Well, you don't look too much the worse for wear."

"Thanks to coffee, and lots of it," she responded, echoing Ryan's earlier statement.

"I knew we should never have left you! I said as much to Greg, but he said Ryan was around to keep an eye on you."

"Oh, he kept an eye on me all right," she said ominously, remembering the way he'd gotten an eyeful of her breasts. "He drove me back to the lodge—" Erica's mouth fell open "—and put me to bed in one of the guest suites."

Erica gave a laughing gasp.

Unflinchingly, she went on with the rest of the story. "I tried to sneak out this morning, but he heard me, plied me with coffee and drove me back to my car—which was still parked in front of the White Fir—and completely failed to take advantage of me in the process."

"Good gracious!"

Kelly sucked in a breath. "I set out to make a point and I fell flat on my face—"

"No, not completely," Erica said, shaking her head. "Instead of confirming you're like your mother, last night might just as well have convinced him of the opposite. After all, you couldn't hold your liquor—" Erica gave her a semiapologetic smile "—and you didn't leave the bar with anyone. I mean, other than Ryan."

Kelly frowned. "He ran the guy off."

Erica raised her eyebrows. "Ryan ran off a guy you were talking to?"

"Not talking to," she corrected. "*Flirting with.* And yes, he ran him off, though he denied it. I don't know what he said to Tate."

At least she *thought* his name had been Tate. Last night continued to be a headache in more ways than one.

Erica laughed. "I ought to tell you my story of Greg running off a guy *I* was flirting with soon after we met."

Kelly sighed and Erica looked at her sympathetically.

"Is it possible that Ryan isn't the black-hearted ogre you think he is?" Erica asked. "Greg liked him."

"Greg's a guy." Then she admitted, "Ryan *was* extraordinarily nice this morning. I couldn't really understand why…"

"Mmm-hmm."

"He wanted to have dinner tonight at Clearwater's."

"And you said?" Erica asked.

"I said yes."

Seven

That night, using directions Kelly had given him, Ryan discovered that Kelly lived in a town house midway between the lodge and Distressed Success.

Her place was in an older development, with a parking space out back and a neat little garden in front.

He rang the doorbell, and when she opened the door, he felt the air whoosh out of him.

She wore a bottle-green velvet jacket that gathered under her breasts and revealed plenty of cleavage. A slim brown skirt and knee-high, high-heeled boots completed her outfit.

He was glad now that he'd dressed more formally

for tonight. He had on beige pants and a striped dress shirt beneath his blazer.

"You look fantastic," he said as his eyes ate her up.

She smiled at him and stepped aside. "Come on in. I just need to grab my purse."

When he'd stepped inside, he immediately realized her house was a showcase for Distressed Success's style.

The front door led directly into a large room with a living-room area at one end and a dining room at the other. A kitchen sat off to one side.

The dining room had a table and sideboard in some sort of distressed finish. A chandelier with multicolored beads that reflected the light hung above the table.

The living room contained a sofa and love seat at right angles to each other. They were covered with a profusion of pillows in different prints and shapes. An etched-glass cabinet stood against one wall and a fireplace was set in another. A tasseled rug partially covered the wood floor.

"If your decorating project at the lodge turns out as well as your house," he said, turning toward her, "I'd say you're well on the path to success."

"*Distressed* Success," she deadpanned.

"Is there any other?" he countered.

She smiled. "I'd offer to show you the rest of the house, but I think we'll be late."

Looking into her eyes, he said, "Next time."

The moment drew itself out between them and he could tell she was thinking about what meaning to attach to his words.

All of them, he wanted to tell her.

Kelly cleared her throat, breaking the mood. "Let me just turn off the lights and make sure I've got my house keys."

As she switched off lamps, he reflected that she'd surprised him last night and proven him wrong, and he wasn't a man used to being surprised—or wrong.

She'd only slept with a guy once or twice. She'd floored him with the admission, though she'd given no sign since that she even remembered what she'd said.

He realized now that she must have been even more affected by growing up with Brenda Hartley than he'd been by being Webb Sperling's son.

Last night she'd even referred to not being able to shake off her mother's history. Now he knew how it had affected her in surprising ways.

Of course, it all meant he'd been wrong about her—wrong to accuse her of being like her mother and wrong to think he had her all figured out.

Sure, the way she'd dressed and acted last night had been at odds with her sexual inexperience, but she seemed to have set out to teach him a lesson.

She'd said she was just living up to the behavior *he* expected of her. Or just maybe, he mused, it was the behavior she was expecting of *herself* that she had fought against.

It also occurred to him now that she might have gotten her start as a designer by making the most of a modest budget while she was growing up. His recollection was that Brenda Hartley was not supposed to have had much money, and rumor around town was that she'd also been an indifferent parent.

When Kelly drifted back to his side, he asked, "Ready?"

She smiled. "Yes."

On the drive over to Clearwater's, they chatted casually about local events. When they got to restaurant, he made sure they were shown to a table with a prime view of the twinkling lights on and around Lake Tahoe.

They talked about innocuous subjects such as the weather and skiing. She'd learned to ski only when she'd moved to Tahoe, he discovered, while he did black-diamond runs to work off steam.

After the waiter arrived and they'd placed their order—she, a salad and veal française, he, a shrimp cocktail and the surf and turf—he sat back and contemplated her.

She had extraordinary features. Her bone structure was exquisite and the combination of full lips and hazel eyes with shades of topaz added a hint of exoticism.

"Why are you staring at me?" She looked back at him with a hint of uncertainty.

"You're beautiful," he said simply. In her case, it was a statement of fact, not flattery.

She looked as if she didn't know how to react. "Thank you," she said eventually.

"I also think you're not completely happy with the fact," he added.

Her eyes lowered to hide her expression. "I don't know what you mean."

"I mean," he said, refusing to let her off the hook, "you don't seem entirely comfortable being Brenda Hartley's daughter."

"About as comfortable as you are being Webb Sperling's son."

He nodded briefly. "I accept that," he said, then he eyed her. "Have you been in touch with him recently?"

"Who?" she asked, cloaking her expression again.

"You know who. Your mother's former lover." He said it unflinchingly, forcing them both to face the fact baldly.

"Why would I tell you?" she countered. "You obviously don't approve."

"I don't like watching anyone make a deal with the devil."

"Some have called *you* ruthless and worse. I *do* read the newspapers like everyone else, you know."

He changed tactics. "Webb Sperling is a philanderer and worse."

She remained silent.

"When I started hearing rumors he was having an affair with your mother," he went on, "I knew it wasn't the first time he'd cheated. But my mother had just gotten diagnosed with stage-three breast cancer. I figured the least the bastard could do was keep his pants zipped while she went through chemo."

She still said nothing, though this time she looked as if she wanted to.

"Did you know about the affair?"

The answer was irrelevant to him now, but curiosity made him ask.

She nodded finally. "My mother has a history of choosing the wrong men at the wrong time, starting with my father—actually, maybe even before that." She paused, then added, "I didn't know him, by the way."

"Your father?"

She nodded again. "Brenda wasn't positive about his identity, but she thought he was an out-of-town salesman visiting Vegas while she worked at a casino."

"Yeah, well, I was legitimate, at least," he drawled. "Webb made sure of *that.* There was no way he was jeopardizing his claim on my mother's millions."

"I saw Webb a couple of times during the affair," she admitted, then wrinkled her nose. "He and Brenda weren't the most discreet of couples."

His lips lifted in sardonic amusement. "You call her *Brenda?*"

"Don't you use *Webb?*"

A dry chuckle escaped him. "Another thing we have in common."

"Brenda didn't like to be reminded she was a mother," Kelly said. "It was bad enough I spelled the end of her aspirations to be a showgirl. Of course, since I'm twenty-eight now, she'd much rather I lied these days and said we were sisters."

"Given what you look like, I don't blame her for that."

"Thank you. At least you got to escape Clayburn and go to Harvard."

"Yeah, except I discovered there's no use trying to outrun your past."

"Easy for you to say," she replied. "You've always had money, power—"

"—and you never have," he finished for her.

"Exactly."

"You know," he said, "I remember driving by the house you lived in with your mother."

She looked surprised. "I didn't even know you knew I existed."

"I knew who you were, all right. The rumor mill in Clayburn made sure of that. As a point of pride, though, I pretended not to recognize you."

"So why did you drive by the house?"

He shrugged. "Curiosity. I was mad as hell with my father that day and drove around aimlessly—"

"—yes, I remember you'd tear through town when you were on break from prep school—"

"—and at some point I figured I'd check out where his latest tart was living."

At her raised eyebrows, he added, "It's what I was thinking at the time. *Tart.*"

"Believe me, I've heard worse said about Brenda."

"Ditto about Webb."

He noticed that a tentative camaraderie had taken hold. "I saw you that day in front of the house, walking home in your ice-cream shop uniform."

"I bet you hated me on sight."

"No," he responded slowly, "I was too consumed by anger at Webb to see past to anything else."

"I *never* saw you come into Sloanie's, and it had the best ice cream in town!"

"I didn't want to run into you." He laughed shortly. "Besides, something as wholesome as ice cream would have ruined my bad-boy image."

"I recall," she said drily. "I'd spot you around town from time to time. Of course, I knew you were Webb Sperling's son, but even if I hadn't, your Jaguar convertible would have been a dead giveaway you were the son of the richest family in town."

He smiled rakishly. "I loved that car."

In the next moment, the waiter arrived with their food, and the conversation moved on to other topics.

But a newfound level of understanding existed between them and Ryan was sure he wasn't the only one who felt it—just as he was sure he wasn't the only one to feel the undercurrent of sexual energy.

Afterward, he drove her home. When he pulled up in front of the town house, she offered, "Would you like to come in…for coffee? Or—" her eyes laughed at him "—tea?"

He felt his lips quirk. "Tea sounds great…for the novelty value."

Inside, they took off their jackets and she deposited her purse on an entry table before heading toward the kitchen.

He followed, and they chatted about current events while she boiled water in an old-fashioned teakettle, packed loose tea into a holder and pulled down some cups and saucers.

When she'd prepared two cups of tea, they walked back into the living room and sat on the couch.

The conversation touched on Tahoe and growth nearby in California, and he recounted amusing bits of Silicon Valley lore.

After a while, he looked around and commented, "This is like being allowed into the inner sanctuary."

"Would you like a tour? You didn't get to see it all before we left for dinner."

He nodded. He was looking forward to uncovering some more of the mystery that was Kelly Hartley.

Besides the living room, dining room and kitchen, the lower level of the house had a laundry room and a small bath with scented candles and a little stained-glass cabinet.

When they went upstairs he discovered the upper level had three rooms and a full bath. There was a guest bedroom with a neat, canopied double bed. Next to the guest bedroom, there was a study that functioned as a workroom and that contained a desk, a sewing machine and shelves full of bolts of fabric.

They came to her bedroom last, and as Ryan sauntered in, he realized he'd been wrong. *This* was the inner sanctuary.

A metal four-poster bed occupied most of the room and was covered with brown-and-aqua bedding. A chandelier with blue glass droplets was suspended over the bed. A floor lamp with a poplin shade stood in one corner. Along one wall stood a mirrored dresser. Along another, there was a vanity table and stool. The room was finished with built-in white shelving behind the bed that held books and photos.

Ryan turned back to Kelly. "It's like seeing your style in its purest form. Wow."

She looked embarrassed but flattered. "Thank you, *I think.*"

"You're welcome."

She glanced out the window. "I just noticed. There's a full moon."

He stood beside her and peered out. "So there is. How about that?"

He glanced down at her and was struck anew with the urge to kiss her.

At the same time, she turned to look up at him, her eyes shadowed.

Slowly, he raised his hands to cup her shoulders and turn her to face him fully. Then he lowered his head and brushed her lips.

She sighed against his mouth and he took the kiss deeper, taking the edge off a hunger that dinner had done nothing to sate.

Eventually, his lips drifted away from her lips to explore the delicate shell of her ear and the hollows of her throat.

She swayed into him and sighed again, her arms locking around his neck.

Finally, however, and with difficulty, he raised his head. With Kelly, he'd have to go slow. He took a deep, head-clearing breath and asked, "What are you doing tomorrow?"

Tomorrow was Sunday, and he knew Distressed Success would be closed.

"I'll be at the lodge," she replied huskily. "Working."

"Good."

He had a surprise for her and, fortunately, the weather for tomorrow called for sunny skies and a clear view.

* * *

"I should be working. This is crazy." Kelly pulled loose strands of hair away from her face in a futile battle with the wind.

Though she had her hair tied back in a ponytail, she knew she'd be struggling to get out knots later on.

Ryan grinned in response to her words, his hair whipped by the wind.

He stood by the sails of the boat, and Kelly thought she'd never seen him so carefree. She could well imagine how he might have been a pirate in another life.

She'd shown up early this morning at the lodge because it was Sunday and she didn't have to be in the shop today. She'd intended to put in a full day's work, setting up additional furnishings that had been previously delivered.

Ryan, however, had had other plans. After they'd worked for three hours, he'd taken the vase she'd been holding and announced they were playing hooky for the rest of the day.

It turned out he'd already had a picnic basket packed and, what's more, he'd rented a sailboat.

She had taken one look outside at the glorious weather and had found it impossible to resist.

Now here they were on the vastness of Lake Tahoe—blue skies overhead accentuated by the occasional lazy puffy white cloud, wavy aqua waters below dotted by the occasional watercraft.

Ryan had rented a sloop, which had a single mast and two sails. Because she'd been on a sailboat just once before in her life, Ryan had taught her the basics of trimming the sails and handling the helm before they'd left the dock.

Once they'd gotten under way, however, Ryan had done most of the work. Except for handling the helm when Ryan trimmed the sails, she was able to sit and enjoy the ride.

"Where did you learn to sail?" she called to him now. Then before he could answer, she added, "No, wait. Let me guess. You took Sailing 101 at prep school."

He flashed a grin. "Good guess, but in fact, I learned to sail right here on Lake Tahoe. It's a place where we vacationed when I was younger."

He'd been to Tahoe regularly?

She tilted her head. "That first day at Distressed Success, you acted as if you were unfamiliar with the area. You asked me where you could find a good meal—"

"I was hitting on you."

A tremor of sexual awareness ran through her as something indefinable, but palpable and strong, passed between them.

Silhouetted against the blue sky, he was breathtakingly handsome. He wore khaki pants and a polo shirt paired with a windbreaker and reflective sunglasses. He looked as if he could have been in an ad for Ralph Lauren.

She hadn't known they'd go sailing, but she was glad now that she put on pants and espadrilles that morning. A windbreaker that they'd found for her at the lodge protected her from cold and damp.

As Ryan again busied himself with the sails, she reflected on the events of the weekend. She hadn't intended to reveal so much during their meal at Clearwater's. Still, she could understand Ryan's anger better now, as well as identify with it since Brenda, like Webb, hadn't been the most responsible parent in the world.

Finished with what he was doing, Ryan came toward her and jumped down to where she sat. "Time for lunch. I'm famished."

She laughed. "I can't believe you prepared a whole picnic basket!"

He grinned slyly. "Gourmet everything…courtesy of the concierge service at one of Tahoe's poshest nouveau places."

Eight

Kelly found that the next week passed in a blur of work, decorating and, above all, Ryan and more Ryan.

By the following weekend, she realized somewhat surprisingly that her work at the lodge was nearly done. She also knew she couldn't have done it without Ryan's help.

She hadn't heard anything more from Webb Sperling, but she pushed the thought aside.

She had time, she told herself. Deep down, though, she knew she didn't want to upset her newfound accord with Ryan.

As she prepared to leave the lodge late that Sunday afternoon, Ryan surprised her by saying, "Why don't you come on in? We'll sit on the deck and watch the sunset."

"I should be getting back." The words flew out of her mouth in automatic response.

"Why?" he asked bluntly. "We both know Distressed Success is closed on Mondays." He smiled. "In fact, since you'll want to be working here tomorrow, it makes sense for you to stay the night."

She felt a strange fluttering sensation in her stomach, then caught the teasing glimmer in his eyes.

"After all," he drawled, "you're already familiar with the guest bedroom."

She held her palms up. "I didn't bring any clothes—"

His smile widened. "Do you really want to hear my solution to that problem?"

She felt herself heat in response. She still wasn't used to his teasing.

The past week had been wonderful, but he hadn't tried to kiss her again. He hadn't done anything, in fact, that could be interpreted as a come-on, even by her fevered imagination.

She, on the other hand, had become attuned to his every breath, every expression, every stretch of hard, lean muscle.

Ryan reached out and touched her arm. "Hey," he said soothingly, "come on. Let's just open a bottle of wine and contemplate the meaning of the universe."

She relaxed a little. "Okay."

Minutes later, they stepped out onto the deck, Ryan holding two wineglasses in one hand and a bottle of red wine in the other.

She tried not to look at the hot tub, remembering how she'd first spotted him at the lodge.

"I can vouch for its relaxing properties," he murmured.

"What?" she asked, startled.

"The hot tub. It's great." He paused, a glimmer in his eyes. "Want to try?"

"No, thanks!"

Her response was immediate and automatic. Just the thought of getting into a hot tub with Ryan Sperling sent her senses into overdrive.

"Don't tell me you've never been in a hot tub," he teased.

"Some of us weren't born into the hot-tub-and-wine set." Then she added, relenting, "In any case, I have nothing to wear."

His eyes crinkled. "Why let a lack of clothing stand in your way?"

At her look of forbearance, he shrugged. "Can't blame a guy for trying." He paused, then added thoughtfully, "I could lend you one of my undershirts and a pair of boxers. You could even keep your bra and underwear on underneath."

His lips twitched. "I *know* how important underpants are to you."

She wondered how much of his sexually charged

teasing she could withstand, then asked suspiciously, "And what will you be wearing?"

"Swim trunks."

"I shouldn't agree to this."

He grinned. "But you are."

They headed back inside. He handed her some clothes and, after they'd both had time to change, she met him on the deck again, padding outside in bare feet and shivering in the cool night air.

Soft jazz filtered out from iPod speakers set up on a table.

He stood holding two full wineglasses and swept her a look from head to toe, his gaze heating. "I had no idea my shirts and boxers could look so sexy."

She flushed. It felt impossibly intimate to be wearing his clothes, albeit over her own.

He'd already started the hot tub, and the tub's jets created frothy water, illuminated from below by recessed lights.

It looked so inviting, she thought as she shivered again.

He set the wineglasses down on a small tray at the side of the tub, then straightened and held his hand out to her. "Come. Let's warm you up."

He warmed *her* just by looking at her with his hot eyes, she wanted to say. Instead, she put her hand in his and stepped into the tub.

"Careful," he cautioned, but she knew she was being anything but—*with him, with anything.*

He followed her and settled on an underwater ledge across from her.

She sighed as the hot tub's jets pounded her gently, massaging her muscles. She closed her eyes and leaned back, relaxing against the tub's side.

"Better?"

"Mmm-hmm."

After a few moments, during which she heard him lift and sip from his wineglass, he instructed, "Look up."

She did, and gazed at the inky black sky. Dozens of little stars twinkled back at her.

"My guess is that you haven't had much time to stargaze in your life," he commented.

"Mmm-hmm."

"Neither have I."

She looked down at him, and asked, "Why do you think Hunter wrote a stipulation in his will that you and his other college buddies have to stay at the lodge?"

"Why didn't he just give the money to charity, you mean?"

She nodded.

"We'd made a promise to one another all those years ago, on a night after too many beers. We'd vowed to become huge successes—on our own, not riding on our families' coattails—and then reunite in ten years. Once Hunter got sick, the rest of us forgot that crazy night. But Hunter never did."

He looked heavenward. "Maybe he knew we'd need to do *this*. And somehow he knew it would be up to him to get us to come here just to take a moment and look up at the stars."

"I guess he was right, because it's been a while since you've taken time to look at the stars."

"Ages," he answered absently, then he lowered his head to look at her. "How about you?"

"Ages," she concurred.

A companionable silence followed. She sipped her wine and looked off into the dark trees, then out at the dark waters of Lake Tahoe.

Finally, she asked, "So you and Hunter were close friends?"

He shrugged. "Yeah. I didn't have siblings, so all six of the guys from college were like brothers to me." A wry smile touched his lips. "We called ourselves the Seven Samurai."

She laughed. "Who came up with that name?"

"Blame it on too many late nights chowing down on bad pizza and watching Kurosawa movies. We studied hard, but partied harder."

"You talk about it as if it's one of the better times in your life."

"It was."

"Did you find it difficult being an only child?"

"Did you?" he countered.

"It was more difficult being Brenda Hartley's daughter."

He raised his wineglass in silent salute. "I felt the same way."

"It was as if the college partying days never ended for Brenda," she elaborated, "except she never went to college...."

"But you did," he prompted.

"Yes," she said, looking at him in surprise. "How did you know?"

He shrugged. "A good guess."

"I worked my way through community college in Reno to get a degree in business administration."

The conversation moved to the challenges of starting a business. Kelly found herself fascinated by the tales he had from his climb to the top of the cable-communications world.

After a while, he said, "Now I have a question for you that I've been wondering about. Why did you settle around Tahoe or, more specifically, Hunter's Landing?"

She sighed. "How I got where I am is a lot less interesting than how you got where you are."

"I'm all ears."

She regarded him. He really did seem genuinely curious. "I knew I had to get out of Clayburn," she said eventually. "I knew I didn't want to go to Vegas, but Reno wasn't too far. Once I found a job in Reno, I enrolled at a community college and, on weekends, I'd take cheap day trips to Tahoe."

She shrugged. "I fell in love with the area and,

since there's a big tourist trade here, not to mention lots of seasonal residents, it seemed like the perfect place to try to open a business."

"You've got good instincts," he said.

They'd both finished their wine by this time and the music had died away, replaced by the stillness of the night.

She looked around. "I could lie in here forever, but I'd be a wrinkled prune!"

"Ready to head in?" he asked.

"I think so."

They'd been having such a relaxed, quiet conversation, she'd started to forget they were barely dressed.

Now, however, she was nervous about emerging from the tub.

He placed the wineglasses and wine bottle to one side on the deck and rose. Water sluiced from his body as he climbed out of the hot tub, and awareness shimmered through her as she got a close-up of sheer male virility.

He turned then and made to help her.

She took his outstretched hand and stood up, stepping on the tub ledge, then out onto the deck.

He picked up a couple of towels and handed one to her.

"Th-thank you," she said, and attributed her stutter to chattering teeth caused by the cold.

Except when her eyes accidentally met his, she'd noticed he was looking fixedly at her body.

She looked down at herself, and realized what he saw.

His white shirt was dripping wet and clung to her like a second skin, defining all her curves. Her nipples, made hard by the cold air, were pronounced against the thin cotton of her bra and his shirt. She looked more top-heavy than she did under her own carefully chosen clothes.

She shivered, and his eyes narrowed.

He dropped his towel and slowly reached up and brushed back wisps of her hair.

Then instead of withdrawing his hand, he trailed the back of it along the curve of her jaw, down her neck and lower....

His hand traced the curve of her breast, then moved up to touch a lock of her hair. "Tempting curves, siren hair."

She sucked in a breath.

He looked as if he was still waging a battle with himself, caught between desire and something else.

"I should hate you," she whispered. It was a desperate last bid to avoid what was happening between them.

"No, you don't. Not really. Not anymore," he whispered back.

"I *want* to hate you."

"I wanted to hate you, too," he admitted without a trace of apology, "but I can't. I want you."

He looked into her eyes, his full of desire, then cupped her neck and drew her near.

He searched her face for a moment before he bent his head and touched his lips to hers.

As she let go of her towel, she thought that this moment had been inevitable since the first time he'd walked into her shop.

If he hadn't discovered who she was, and she hadn't found out who he was, they'd probably have reached this point long before now.

His lips claimed hers in a deep, searching kiss. Her body came up flush against his, molding to him, seeking welcoming heat where before there had been just cold.

Her hand moved to the back of his head, pulling him down to her, and she kissed him back, feeding their passion.

A voice inside her head insisted this was wrong. But the voice of scruples was faint, drowned out by the strength of their desire.

He made her feel vibrant and alluring and full of life. The clothes between them warmed from the heat of their desire.

Moments went by before he finally lifted his head and breathed deep.

"I want you," he stated baldly.

"Yes."

He searched her face. "Yes?"

"Make love to me," she breathed, throwing caution to the wind.

It was all the encouragement he seemed to need.

He bent and scooped her up in his arms. "Let's get inside. It's freezing."

He stepped into the house and crossed the great room to the staircase. He took the stairs deliberately, not showing the least exertion from carrying her up.

When they got to the upper level, he went down the hall and into the master suite, setting her down near the bed.

As he lowered her feet to the floor, she brushed against him, doing a slow slide to a want that went bone deep.

"Kiss me," he said, and she complied because it was the only thing she felt she could do.

The kiss went on and on. Their labored breathing filled the stillness of the room and their bodies moved against each other, straining to be closer.

Liquid warmth pooled between her legs.

He pulled his lips away from hers finally and groaned against her mouth. "I want you badly."

"Yes." She felt the same way. A faint tremor shook her hand as she raked it through his hair.

He sat back on the bed and bent to take the tip of one breast into his mouth, groaning as he did so and bending her backward.

She gasped and grasped his shoulders in order to

anchor herself. The sensation of him heating her wet and tender flesh was delicious. "Ryan…"

When his mouth moved away, she was burning with hunger for him.

He pulled the shirt over her head and she raised her arms to assist him. Then he tugged down the boxers she was wearing—*his* boxers—and did the same for her panties. Both pieces of underwear dropped to the floor. Then he pulled her down on the bed for another searing kiss.

When her hand accidentally brushed against him, she stroked his erection and he groaned. Finally, when it seemed as if he couldn't take any more, he pulled his swim trunks off.

She wrapped her hand around him without invitation and his breath hissed out.

A faint smile touched her lips. It felt wonderful to have Ryan Sperling in her grasp, literally, and on his knees, figuratively.

"What are you smiling at?" he asked.

"Nothing," she denied, but caught the sudden urge to tease him. "Just thinking about giving you pleasure…having you in the palm of my hand—"

He tilted his head, his eyes heavy lidded. "Oh, yeah?"

In the next instant, he pushed her back on the enormous bed and came down beside her, anchoring her.

She squealed and he nuzzled her breasts.

"That first day at Distressed Success," she said, striving to keep her train of thought, "before I knew who you were, I was immediately attracted to you."

He lifted his head, his expression roguish. "I wanted you like crazy."

Her eyes widened. "You did?"

He nodded. "I already admitted I was hitting on you. Of course I had the hots for you."

"I thought—"

"What?" He smiled. "You think I hit on every young female entrepreneur selling mismatched china?"

She pretended to look offended.

With a grin, he looked at her bra and slid a finger under the band. "Are you going to take this off for me?"

"It's front closure."

"In that case—" He raised himself up and undid the clasp between her breasts, allowing them to spill free.

"You're beautiful," he said reverently, tracing the outline of one breast.

Then he kissed her and caressed her all over, bringing her to a fever pitch. When he dipped a finger into her damp heat, she went dizzy with sensation.

"Ryan," she said hoarsely.

But he pressed, making rapid little movements, like the beating of butterfly wings.

She moaned, mindless with pleasure.

Then, all at once, she went up and over and into

the vortex, her grip on his arm the only thing anchoring her to the world.

He pressed his mouth against her damp heat, making her gasp again and jerk, even as her fingers threaded through his hair.

She felt the tension within her build again and she trembled against him. Turning her head to one side, she pulled a pillow toward her, trying to muffle the way he made her feel.

Within moments, however, he pulled the pillow from her grasp.

"I want to hear you," he said hoarsely.

And then he enjoyed her until she felt liquid fire dance along her nerve endings.

Her release was fiery and rapid, bringing tears to her eyes.

She lay limp afterward and thought dimly that her limited experience had not compared to this…had not prepared her for Ryan Sperling.

He pressed kisses to her inner thighs, then levered himself up off the bed. He pulled open a dresser drawer and retrieved a foil packet.

"Because you just never know when you'll need it," he explained.

"I'll do it," she responded, and watched his eyes flare.

She'd never done this before, but he made her feel daring and bold.

She took the foil packet from him, but when he

lay back on the bed, instead of rolling the protection on him, she pleasured him with her mouth.

He tensed with surprise, then relaxed and groaned. "Kelly…"

She heard the warning in his voice but, knowing she was undermining his control, she kept on going.

"I'm about to lose it," he said hoarsely.

When she raised her head, he gave her a quick hard kiss.

"Bold in bed," he said, smiling. "I like that."

It took them a long time to roll the protection on him. In the end, neither of them could wait any longer.

He rolled her under him and parted her thighs. Then, holding her gaze, he slid into her slowly and came down into her arms.

The buildup was slow—and he toyed with her, increasing her pleasure—but when her release came, it was in a rush of sensation so that she gasped and cried out, grasping his hips as she moved against him.

His release came on the heels of hers and he spilled himself inside her.

She held him afterward, knowing that in this moment he was totally hers.

Nine

When Kelly woke the next morning, she glanced over and blinked. Ryan looked back at her, his hair tousled.

She'd done that, she realized, heat rising. Last night, she'd raked her fingers through his hair, and so much more.

"Good morning," he said.

"Morning," she said, suddenly unsure of herself. She tried to glance at the clock on the bedside table.

"It's only eight," he said. "Plenty of time for you to get to work, which, in any case, is right here." He smiled. "Lucky you. You can just roll out of bed and be on the job."

Last night had been what she'd imagined sex was supposed to be. She'd pictured it in her mind countless times. And it had finally become a reality with Ryan Sperling.

"Last night was incredible," he said, as if reading her mind.

A pleasurable thrill shot through her. It had been wonderful for her, too, but she wasn't as experienced in bed as she was sure Ryan was.

"It'd been a while for me," he stated.

She looked at him in surprise. *She* was the one who'd been all but celibate most of her adult life.

"Really? Why?" she asked.

"You could say I've been consumed with other things…"

"It's been a while for me, too," she admitted.

"Yeah, I know." Under the bed sheets, his hand trailed along her leg.

He knew? Had she been so obviously rusty and inexperienced last night? She felt heat stain her cheeks.

She looked at him quizzically. "How did you know? Was I so obviously a novice?"

He shook his head and gave her a quick kiss. "No, but that night at the White Fir, when I got you home, and before you drifted off to sleep—"

She felt herself tense. She'd wondered whether she'd forgotten some key details from that night.

"—you mentioned you'd been with only one guy before, and then only a couple of times."

"I did?" Apparently, when she was tipsy, she relished divulging her innermost secrets.

His lips quirked. "You'll recall your conversation was a little, ah, disjointed, that night. I got you into bed and a second before you fell asleep, you said something about never having spent the entire night with a man before, though of course—" his eyes crinkled "—I was getting you into bed only in the most literal sense."

Her brows drew together. "So you knew this when you slept with me last night?"

A smile rose to his lips again, even as the heat rose to her face.

"Yeah," he said.

His words landed with the force of an explosion— at least to her. Looking at him, she knew he had no clue.

The rat, she thought.

He'd known all along just how inexperienced she was. No wonder he'd changed his tune after that night at the White Fir.

What had he claimed as the reason behind his change in attitude? The realization that *we all make mistakes?*

Well, *she'd* made a mistake—starting with sleeping with him last night!

She threw back the bedcovers and got out of bed.

"Where are you going?" he asked.

He continued to look guileless—his tone and expression relaxed and satisfied—and it fueled her anger.

She grabbed her clothes from where she'd put them on a nearby chair last night and decided to give him a clue.

"So I was an easy target?" she demanded. "Ripe for the picking because you knew I'd gone so long without, hmm?"

He sat up, suddenly alert. "No. I explained I haven't had any, either—"

She waved a hand. "Yes, I know. *In ages.* All the more reason for you to have been thrilled to find a soft target. I just fell into your lap, didn't I?"

He smiled roguishly. "Well, if you want to put it that way—"

"No wonder you seemed so willing suddenly to overlook the fact I was Brenda Hartley's daughter!"

"Don't dare bring your mother into it," he said, no longer joking as he rose from the bed.

She stomped to the nearby bathroom and slammed the door and locked it.

"Damn it, come back here so we can talk about this!"

She ignored him.

"Kelly!" He knocked on the door and twisted the knob. "Come on out."

Methodically, she dressed, while he continued to knock and pound.

"All right," he said eventually. "I'm not having

this conversation through the bathroom door. I'm going downstairs to make some coffee and wait for you to calm down."

She *was* calm, she wanted to tell him. In fact, she was thinking more lucidly than she had all weekend.

He hadn't mentioned he knew her sexual history, or lack thereof, until *after* he'd gotten her into bed.

She thought he'd started seeing *her*—really seeing her—for the whole of who she was. Instead, he'd seen no more than a potential bed buddy, convinced by nothing more than her sexual history.

She couldn't believe she'd started falling for him. She was such an idiot.

She dressed quickly, then took a deep breath. She would march out of the house without letting Ryan persuade her otherwise. He couldn't be trusted.

She would just have to chalk up today as a loss as far as finishing the job at the lodge went. Later, she could figure out how she was going to finish up her decorating work without coming into contact with Ryan. She'd just have to come to an arrangement with him to be at the lodge while he was out.

Taking another deep breath, she opened the bathroom door and looked around.

The room was empty and her eyes strayed to the huge bed. The rumpled and twisted sheets were a reminder of last night.

Resolutely looking away, she stole out of the room and crept down the stairs.

This was the second time she was trying to sneak away, and while she was prepared for Ryan to intercept her, she preferred not to have a scene.

When she'd made it down to the lower level, she sighed with relief.

She quietly opened the front door…and her heart leapt to her throat.

"Brenda?" Her question came out as a gasp.

Her mother, who had been surveying the drive, turned to face her.

Brenda's bright red lips curved into a smile. "Hello, tootsie. I was just about to ring the doorbell."

Kelly felt her heart race. No, no, no, she wanted to scream. Not here, not now.

"What are you doing here?" she squeaked.

Brenda's smile dimmed. "I went by your house, but you weren't there. When I tried your cell and couldn't reach you, I called Erica. She was out with the kids, but Greg told me you might be here."

"I—"

"Aren't you going to invite me in?"

"Kelly."

Ryan's voice sounded behind her and, as if in a nightmare, Kelly watched Brenda look past her, just as she herself turned to see Ryan coming into the foyer.

All three of them froze.

Ryan stared at the woman in the doorway, and his lips thinned. Even if he hadn't seen her before, it wouldn't have been hard to figure out who she was. She looked like an older version of Kelly.

He'd come to iron things out with Kelly—because last night had been fantastic, and because now that he'd found her, he wasn't letting her go. Instead, he was confronted by one of the last people he wanted to see.

"Brenda," Kelly said, "this isn't a good time—"

Ignoring her, Brenda sashayed in, looking from her daughter to Ryan and back. "I see I'm interrupting something."

She looked Ryan up and down in frank appraisal, making his skin feel tight with angry tension.

"What makes you think so?" Kelly asked, addressing her mother.

Ryan could have told her that her high-pitched, slightly hysterical voice was a dead giveaway.

Brenda lifted her hand, with its fire-engine red nails, and rubbed a lock of Kelly's hair between her fingers.

"Bed hair," she said succinctly.

Kelly flushed, then looked helplessly at Ryan.

He approached slowly, aiming for a casual stance. "Kelly's sister, I presume?"

Brenda gave a tinkling laugh, as if she found his question highly amusing. "I see you inherited your father's charm."

She turned to her daughter. "I admit being surprised, however, that you picked Webb's son as your…playmate."

Kelly drew in an audible breath. "You know who he is?"

Brenda flashed a hard smile. "I make it my business to keep up with all of Clayburn's current and past illustrious citizens." Then she looked at Ryan again. "However, the photos I've seen of you in the local papers don't do you justice."

If the comment had come from anyone else, Ryan figured he'd have been flattered. But this was Brenda Hartley. Clayburn's erstwhile sexpot. His father's former mistress. *Kelly's mother.*

The last thought brought him up short.

Kelly looked as if she were in agony.

Brenda apparently noticed, too, because she flashed a saucy smile at her daughter. "There's no need to look panicked, Kelly. I'm just glad you're having some—" she paused and gave Ryan a sweeping look "—fun. I was starting to worry about you, toots."

"Why are you here?" Kelly asked, looking as if she wanted the ground to open up and swallow her.

Brenda focused her attention back on her daughter. "Why, to see you, of course!" She leaned in and kissed the air next to Kelly's cheek. "And you know, I may need the teeny, tiniest—" she indicated how much by a small space between her index finger and thumb "—little loan."

Brenda glanced at Ryan, her expression shrewd. "On the other hand, maybe these days you can afford more than a *little* loan...."

Ryan decided he'd heard enough. It was time he took over the situation.

"Come on in, Brenda," he said.

"We're just leaving, actually," Kelly said quickly.

"No, you're not."

Brenda clapped her hands. "Oh, I love a man who takes charge."

His eyes clashed with Kelly's, before he looked back at Brenda. "Coffee?"

"I'd love some," Brenda responded.

"Okay, then *I'm* leaving," Kelly said.

He shrugged and turned toward the back of the house. He had some negotiating to do with Brenda Hartley, and if Kelly wasn't around, so much the better.

Brenda started to follow him toward the back of the house.

"Fine," Kelly said in exasperation behind them. "In that case, I'm going back upstairs to take a shower. Let me know when your coffee break is over."

Back in the kitchen, he gestured Brenda toward a seat at the counter and removed the coffee carafe from its holder.

"How do you take it?" he asked.

"Black, no sugar."

"I figured."

He checked himself, waiting for the hate to kick in.

For years, he'd loathed Brenda Hartley for having an affair with Webb.

Somewhat surprisingly, however, all he felt at the moment was a cool detachment. He was prepared to deal with her in the same way he'd dealt with everything that had stood in his path to date—with unemotional, clear-eyed calculation.

He set a coffee cup down in front of Brenda and asked without preamble, "So why'd you take up with Webb?"

She sipped her coffee and took her time responding. "He was rich—" she gave a throaty laugh "—and good in bed."

"He's slime. His wife was dying."

Brenda shrugged and suddenly she looked every one of her years. "For men like Webb, life's too short to forgo the kicks." She wagged a finger suddenly. "But don't think he's the only married man to wander. At least he was generous with the perks."

"I just bet he was," Ryan replied drily, leaning back against the counter and folding his arms. "But that generosity ended a long time ago and now you're back to scavenging."

Brenda's brows snapped together. "I do *not*—"

"How much?" he interrupted.

She stopped. "How much what?"

"How much do you need from Kelly?"

Brenda sat back, a slow smile spreading across her face. "I like a man who's willing to talk business."

* * *

The next morning, when Kelly showed up for work at Distressed Success, Erica was waiting for her.

"Well," Erica said, as Kelly set about getting ready to open the store for business, "how did your date with Ryan go?"

"Where do I begin?" Kelly responded drily. "Brenda showed up as I was trying to sneak out of the lodge and away from Ryan yesterday morning."

Erica's eyes widened and her jaw dropped. It was one of the few times Kelly had seen her at a loss for words.

"Wow…I'm not sure I know where to begin," Erica said slowly. "Brenda's in Tahoe? *You slept with him?* And what do you mean you were sneaking away?"

Kelly filled her in on the events of the weekend, omitting, however, some of the more salacious details. She ended with, "No wonder he changed his tune after that night at the White Fir!"

"Well," Erica said, "you're sure leading a more exciting life than I am. Mine's a merry-go-round of work and kids. Yours is more interesting than watching the afternoon soaps."

"I'd opt for *boring* in a heartbeat."

Erica laughed. "Not with a yummy beefcake like Ryan Sperling around, you shouldn't."

"Haven't you heard what I said? His whole aim was to try to get me into bed."

"Yeah, that was more or less Greg's primary goal in life when we first met."

Kelly looked at Erica, a seed of doubt was sown. Her friend had been married close to ten years, she had more experience with men and she didn't look nearly as condemning of Ryan.

"Are you saying Ryan isn't wrong?" Kelly asked.

"No, he's a rat," Erica responded cheerfully, "but he's a *man,* so the behavior's understandable—predictable, even."

"Thanks for the tip," she said drily.

"Since Brenda is in town, remind me to hide some of the new stock that came in," Erica replied. "Last time she was here, she made off with a new jewelry box and a small vase."

As it turned out, Kelly spent the next days having Brenda as her houseguest—and trying to forget Ryan Sperling.

Luckily, she was forced to spend a significant amount of time at Distressed Success. Brenda, fortunately, was more than happy to entertain herself with the attractions of Tahoe and its casinos.

As she got ready for work on Thursday morning, Kelly thought with relief about the fact that her work at the lodge was nearly done. The furnishings had arrived for all the bedrooms, and except for waiting for an odd piece or two and hanging up a few more pictures, she was finished.

Just as she and Ryan were *finished,* she thought with remaining anger—and a pang or two. Soon, she'd never have to see him again. Her job at the lodge would be done and his month in Hunter's Landing would be up.

He hadn't tried to contact her since she'd left the lodge three days ago and, as much as she hated to admit it, it hurt that he hadn't. She could only suppose that now that he knew she was clued in to his game, he'd moved on to other amusements.

Three days ago, when she'd come back down the stairs at the lodge after freshening up, she'd encountered Brenda in the foyer.

Not wanting another confrontation with Ryan, she'd asked sharply, "Ready?"

"Aren't you going to kiss Ryan goodbye?" Brenda had responded, a gleam in her eye.

"We'll be seeing each other again soon, I'm sure," she'd hedged. "He'll understand."

"Take it from me, tootsie," Brenda had advised. "If you want to keep a man, *never* leave without saying goodbye."

Thinking about Brenda's words now, Kelly sighed. The advice said it all about her relationship with her mother.

She glanced toward her bedroom doorway as Brenda appeared, as if on cue.

"I'm heading out," Brenda announced.

"What?"

Brenda had gotten back so late last night, Kelly hadn't seen her—she'd already been asleep.

She glanced down now at the carry-on bag at her mother's side. "Where are you going?"

Brenda laughed. "Home. You didn't think I was staying forever, did you?"

Clayburn was home again to Brenda these days, though her mother led such a peripatetic existence, Kelly wondered how long the current state of affairs would last.

She finished buttoning the jacket of her green pantsuit. "I'm just surprised, that's all. You said nothing about leaving yesterday."

Her mother waved a hand negligently. "You know I prefer living life in the moment. It makes things so much more *interesting.*"

Kelly helped her mother take her luggage outside, then paused beside Brenda's car.

"You never told me how much you needed," she said, remembering suddenly Brenda's request when she'd shown up at the lodge earlier in the week.

"How much I needed for what?"

Kelly sighed. "When you arrived, you mentioned you needed a small loan."

Brenda gave a throaty laugh and waved a hand dismissively. "Oh, *that*. It's not necessary anymore."

Kelly frowned. "What do you mean it's not necessary? Did you win at the slot machines?"

Brenda laughed again. "Well…I suppose that's what I *should* say."

"*Should?*"

Brenda leaned in and lowered her voice, though no one else was around. "Your *boyfriend* asked me to keep this quiet, but what the hell? You *should* know." She seemed to pause for dramatic effect, her eyes alight. "He *gave* me the money."

"*Ryan?*"

Brenda straightened, a satisfied look on her face, and she patted Kelly's cheek. "You have that man eating out of the palm of your hand. I always knew you were a smart girl."

"How much did he give you?" she blurted.

Part of her didn't want to know—dreaded knowing, actually—but the other part knew she had to find out.

Brenda hesitated. "Five thousand."

"*Dollars?*"

Brenda laughed again. "What else is there? I knew he could afford more, but I also knew asking for more might make him suspicious. After all, I did say I needed a *small* loan from you."

"How could you?" she asked, the question coming out like a wail. "How could you take money from him?"

Brenda sighed impatiently. "Why should I have turned him down?"

"Didn't you think you might be creating…obligations for me?"

"Well, considering you're already sleeping with him," Brenda replied tartly, "I don't see how *that* could be the case."

Kelly opened and shut her mouth. It was useless. Arguing with Brenda was like banging her head against a brick wall. They came at things from two different sets of assumptions—two different worldviews. She should have learned that by now.

"How did he get the money to you?" she demanded. "Not even someone as rich as Ryan carries around that much cash."

"He had his people wire some money to me."

"No wonder you had to stay in the area for a few days!"

"Listen, tootsie," Brenda replied dismissively, "I've really got to go." She checked her watch. "I have someone waiting for me at the casino."

As Brenda gave her a quick kiss, Kelly thought that without a doubt the *someone* was male and with money to burn.

After she'd deposited her mother's suitcase in the trunk of her ancient Mercedes—which she knew for a fact Brenda had bought for a song at some dismal used car lot—she watched her mother pull away from the town house.

Then she went back inside, closed the front door, and braced her hand against the wall for support.

What had Ryan done? *And why?*

She tried to sort through her jumble of emotions.

On some level, she *was* grateful. After all, Brenda would have asked her for the money, otherwise.

But she was also *upset.*

She didn't want rich men doing favors for her. It made her feel like Brenda. It made her feel cheap.

Oh, sure, she'd sort of accepted a favor from Webb Sperling. But that was different. It was an even exchange. She had confidence in the strength of her designs—it was just a question of getting her goods into the hands of the right buyers.

This situation with Ryan was different. She felt bought. He'd out-and-out paid off her mother.

For her, her heart whispered, before she could avoid it.

And that was the other reason this situation was different, she told herself. Because it was Ryan, not Webb, who was involved. Part of why she'd felt so betrayed when she'd realized what his motivation had been for sleeping with her was that it *did* matter to her what Ryan thought of her.

She had her pride, she told herself—even though her heart whispered again, telling her that there was something more than *pride* involved here.

Somehow, she had to repay him.

She racked her brain, then smiled as an idea eventually came to mind.

As soon as she got to work, she had a call to make to Webb Sperling.

Ten

"Since Oliver is on board, we're set to go," Dan said.

Ryan watched his attorney pull paperwork out of his briefcase. They were sitting in the lodge's office loft, the morning sun coming in through the windows.

Dan had driven over from Silicon Valley, where El Ray Technology was based, as soon as the sun had come up. Now, he set contracts out on the table before them.

"Everyone has signed," Dan explained, "so I just need your signature before I—" he smiled fleetingly "—send out some big checks."

"I want this wrapped up ASAP," Ryan said, checking his watch. "It's already Thursday. I'd like to make this transfer public by early next week *before* someone leaks the news to the press."

He wanted to call the shots in this situation. He'd decide when and how Webb Sperling found out that the trap had been sprung.

"There's a confidentiality clause in all the contracts—"

"Yes, I know," Ryan said, cutting him off, "but we're talking about the Sperlings here. Any one of them is capable of wreaking havoc at the last minute."

"It'll be done," Dan replied, as Ryan leaned forward and began to sign. "I know you want to start concentrating on other things—like El Ray's acquisitions in foreign markets."

El Ray was in the beginning stages of courting cable companies in South and Central America for a partnership or buyout. All the more reason, Ryan thought, to get this issue of Sperling, Inc. wrapped up and for this idyll in Hunter's Landing to come to a close.

"In the meantime," Dan continued, "I've already drafted a letter to Webb, warning him his executive authority has ended and that all pending contracts negotiations and other matters are to be suspended."

Ryan thought about Kelly's contract. There was a time not too long ago when he would have made it a priority to pull the plug on Distressed Success as soon as he got control of Sperling, Inc.

He doubted Kelly had had a chance to sew up a

deal with Sperling stores—she certainly hadn't given any indication to the effect during the time they'd spent together.

Knowing his father, Ryan figured he'd just passed the matter along to underlings and gone on with his golf game or whatever the heck else he did these days.

As Dan began to drone on about the contract particulars, Ryan's mind stayed on Kelly.

It had been three days since he'd last seen her. Three days since the confrontation with Brenda.

In that time, he'd been tied up with his bid to get control of Sperling, Inc. In addition, he hadn't wanted to go by Kelly's place to hash things out if Brenda was still hanging around.

And, he admitted, he'd expected Kelly to put in an appearance at the lodge before now, no matter how much she might want to continue to avoid him.

She'd surprised him, however, by managing to stay away from the decorating job for three consecutive days.

She was probably occupied with her unexpected houseguest, he told himself. But another part of him acknowledged that there was no reason to think she'd softened toward him since Monday.

Yes, her sexual inexperience, once he'd found out about it, had put a whole new spin on things. But contrary to what she believed, it wasn't her inexperience in and of itself that had attracted him. Rather, it was because it was further, definitive proof of what he'd been seeing signs of all along, but hadn't allowed himself to acknowledge: Kelly was far different from her mother.

He had no intention of leaving Hunter's Landing without telling her so—just as soon as this damn issue with Sperling, Inc. was concluded.

He was going to have it out with her *and* have her. *Again and again,* until they were both mindless with pleasure.

"Have you heard?" Erica asked, when she showed up for her shift around lunchtime on Tuesday.

"Heard what?" Kelly replied distractedly.

She was doing some record keeping at her desk in her office at the back of Distressed Success.

She'd promised herself today would be the day she faced the music by going back to the lodge. She'd also just run out of excuses, because Erica had shown up and could cover for her at the shop.

"Ryan Sperling has taken over Sperling department stores and ousted his father from his role as CEO and chairman of the board!"

Kelly's head jerked up. "What? Where did you hear that?"

"I heard it on the radio on the drive over," Erica said. "You called Webb just in time."

Kelly pulled out her computer keyboard, and with trembling fingers, she did a Google search for Ryan Sperling and Sperling department stores.

A slew of hits came up, including a bunch of local news stories from the last few hours.

She clicked on the first site listed and, when the article came up, scanned it rapidly.

It appeared Ryan had bought ownership shares in Sperling, Inc. from various family members, giving him a majority stake.

His first order of business had been to remove his father from the chairmanship of the board and to strip him of his title of CEO.

She sank back against the chair weakly, trying to digest the import of Ryan's takeover, her mind racing. Out front, she heard the shop door open and close, and knew they had another customer.

Rotten timing, she thought, then rose and said to Erica, "I'll get this one."

At the very least, the customer might help take her mind off the bombshell that had just landed in her lap.

She walked out to the front of the store, a polite smile on her face. "Can I help—"

She came to a halt.

There facing her was none other than Webb Sperling.

Webb Sperling fixed her with a dim smile as he looked her up and down. "Hello, Kelly. You're the spitting image of your mother."

Kelly felt her own smile fade.

Webb's eyes were pale—a washed-out blue, she remembered thinking once—and he looked as if he'd put on a good fifteen or twenty pounds since she'd last seen him more than a decade ago. At around six feet, he was tall and imposing—but also paunchy and balding, his complexion florid.

"What are you doing here?" she blurted.

Rather than answer, he sauntered farther into the store. "I suppose you've heard the news."

"This morning," she responded shortly. What did one say to someone who'd just lost control of his company and been ousted from his position? *Condolences? I'm sorry?*

Webb glanced around. "Nice little boutique you have here."

"Thank you," she said, "but I doubt it's what brings you by."

"Actually," he drawled, "I'm on vacation in the area—"

A *forced* vacation, Kelly thought.

"—and I thought you'd be able to tell me where to find Ryan. This morning, he wasn't at the fancy log house he's staying at nearby."

She tensed. "Why do you thing I would know?"

"There's no need to be coy, sugar," Webb responded. "Brenda's filled me in on the fact that you and Ryan are lovers."

She sucked in a breath and the look on Webb Sperling's face said he knew he'd struck a direct hit.

She opened her mouth to reply just as the front door opened and Ryan walked in.

Webb turned, coming face-to-face with the man Kelly had thought never to see in her shop again.

"Well, well," Webb drawled, "I see I'm interrupting a rendezvous."

"What the hell are you doing here?" Ryan shot back.

Webb's lips twisted. "Isn't it obvious? I'm here to congratulate you on your recent coup."

"The element of surprise was part of my plan," Ryan responded coolly.

"If you'd just waited, it would have all been yours one day."

"It's mine now." Ryan's jaw hardened.

"You always were the impatient type."

Kelly looked back and forth from father to son, fascinated despite herself by the exchange.

"I'd been planning on retiring," Webb mused, looking out the store windows. "Roxanne wants to be able to travel and not be tied down by business." He looked back at Ryan. "We may even spend part of the year right here in Tahoe."

"Is that the story you're spinning for the press?" Ryan said scornfully.

"It's the truth."

Webb adopted a look of such open sincerity, Kelly almost believed him herself despite the fact that his declarations were obviously a face-saving gesture, now that he'd been unceremoniously ousted from Sperling, Inc.

No wonder the man had been such a successful and clandestine adulterer for years, she thought— he created his own reality.

"Like hell," Ryan retorted, then his eyes shot to her. "When did he get here?"

Her gaze met and clashed with his. "Just now."

He looked back at Webb. "Where's the wife?"

"Roxanne?"

"If she's the one you're still married to," he responded icily.

"She's back at the hotel. I didn't think she needed to be here."

"More likely, you didn't want her finding out any unsavory details she might not be aware of already," Ryan sneered. "After all, a visit to the daughter of your former mistress might set off alarm bells, particularly for a woman with a well-honed sense of self-preservation like Roxanne."

Kelly almost laughed.

Webb managed to look wounded, then cagey. "The apple doesn't fall far from the tree. According to Brenda, you're screwing her daughter."

Ryan's eyes blazed. "My relationship with Kelly has nothing, *nothing,* in common with yours and Brenda's, no matter what the hell that relationship is these days."

Webb's eyes gleamed. "Brenda and I have stayed

close friends." He threw a quick glance at Kelly. "I recommend it with one's former lovers, by the way. You never know when they'll prove useful, especially when a family *affair* looks to be repeating itself."

Ryan's expression turned stony. "You're out," he gritted. "Out of a job, out of Sperling, Inc. and out of here."

Webb laughed. "You're quite protective of your little chickadee." He looked Kelly up and down, then murmured, "I can understand the attraction."

Ryan's fists clenched, but Webb turned toward the door.

"Roxanne and I plan to take an extended European vacation," Webb informed them.

"Of course," Ryan replied acidly, "you'll want to take a long vacation until all of your socialite friends move on to the next piece of gossip." He paused, then added, "Is that why you were tracking me down? To let me know how you were going to spin this?"

"And there are the thoroughbreds to be raised and traded, of course," Webb went on, as if he hadn't heard.

"The horse farm never interested me."

"You took after your mother's side of the family in that way," Webb replied, shaking his head as he walked to the shop's entrance, "but it's heartening to see you've inherited my taste in women."

With that parting shot, Webb opened the store's front door and left.

Ryan turned back to face her.

Before he could say anything, however, the door to the store opened again and a customer walked in.

Kelly smiled—with relief, really—at her unexpected customer, and moved forward. "May I help you?"

As she walked past Ryan, she murmured, "We can't talk now."

Moments later, as she was directing the customer to a display of furniture knobs, she noticed Ryan leaving.

She sighed, then watched as Erica emerged from the back room.

"You heard?" she asked in a low voice.

Erica nodded. "But with all the fireworks going off around here, I was afraid to come out of the storeroom."

"I wish I'd been back there with you."

That night, Tahoe received buckets of rain. It was one of the most powerful thunderstorms in recent memory.

Kelly sat in her living room, contemplating the rivulets of water cascading down her windows.

She sat, still in her work clothes, worn out by the drama that had played out at Distressed Success earlier.

Even if she'd been brave enough to face Ryan

tonight—even if the storm hadn't kept her home—
she wouldn't have known what to say to him.

Yes, he was maddeningly self-assured, arrogant even, with looks that were too sinful to waste
on a hard-nosed corporate raider. But he was
more than that.

She thought about the way he'd taken time to
help her decorate the lodge, patiently waiting while
she contemplated something, happy to move things
if she changed her mind completely.

She remembered how he'd gotten her back safely
and tucked into bed the night she'd put away too
much at the White Fir.

She thought about the wind ruffling his hair that
day on the sailboat on Lake Tahoe.

She even thought about, yes, how he'd given
money to Brenda.

And she realized that, whether she liked it or not,
she had fallen for him. It was why she'd been so hurt
when she'd thought he'd slept with her just because
she might have been an easy lay, convinced by nothing
more than her sexual experience that she was *okay*.

She wanted to be *more* to him. She wanted him to
appreciate all of her. Her temper had had time to cool
these last few days, allowing her to realize as much.

Tears threatened suddenly, but she held them back.

It was useless to feel the way she did, because
Ryan didn't feel the same way about her. To him, she
was just a fling during his enforced stay in Tahoe.

There was no way Ryan could want a more permanent association with the woman who remained, unalterably, Brenda Hartley's daughter.

She even *looked* like Brenda. He wouldn't want to wake up over the years, look over at the next pillow and be reminded again and again of the woman that his father had been sleeping with during his mother's last months.

The sound of the doorbell startled her from her reverie and she wondered with some unease about who could be ringing her doorbell in the middle of a thunderstorm.

She peered out her living-room window.

Dimly, she could make out a man's form.

He must have seen a movement, because he turned to face her and she saw it was Ryan.

Her heart began to pound.

She got up and moved to the door, unlocking and opening it.

"Yes?" she asked.

Droplets ran down from the brim of his hat.

"Can I come in?" he asked.

Without responding, she moved aside and he stepped inside.

While she closed the door to the wind and wet, he pulled off his hat and jacket.

Turning back to him, she said, "Let me take those."

He handed them to her, and she deposited them on a nearby coatrack.

After that, she folded her arms and walked farther into the house. He followed.

She turned when she reached the middle of the living room. "Can I offer you a drink?" She nodded at her cup. "I just made a pot of tea."

It seemed ridiculous to be offering him a drink, but it served to cover the terrible tension.

"Thanks, but I'm fine." He looked at her closely. "You look tearful."

She'd been so surprised by the sound of the doorbell, she hadn't thought about her appearance.

"Allergies," she fibbed.

He walked toward her. "I don't think so."

"I can't imagine why you're here," she said quickly.

"Can't you?" he responded obliquely.

Her chin came up. "Come to tell me that your first order of business as the new head of Sperling, Inc. is to cut off Distressed Success?"

"I think you know the answer to that question."

Her lips parted.

His expression remained indecipherable. "I'm not willing to walk away from the bargaining table—yet."

She wrapped her arms around herself. She longed for the return of her midnight lover of tender caresses and passionate kisses, but the man in front of her wore a mask of inscrutability.

"Provided you can meet a few conditions," he said, "I think we're in business."

Her heart pounded. "Such as?"

"The first thing anyone would need to know," he said, "is whether you have any brand recognition."

Her spirits sank. "Well, not really—"

"It doesn't have to be nationwide," he supplied helpfully. "It could just be local. Say a small place like Hunter's Landing?"

She nodded. "People in Hunter's Landing definitely recognize Distressed Success."

The truth was, it was a laughably small place to rely on for brand recognition.

"What about meeting demand?" he asked. "Who are your suppliers?"

She felt a spark of hope. Here she was on firmer ground. "I have some manufacturers right here on the west coast. I know they're reliable. They've produced samples for me ahead of schedule in the past. Plus, I found them on recommendations and I know they produce goods for some of the major department store brands."

"Even Sperling stores?"

"Even Sperling," she confirmed.

"What about gross-profit margins?" he went on. "Department stores usually look for around forty-five percent, but—" he stopped and looked at her thoughtfully "—that's negotiable."

"How negotiable?" she asked suspiciously.

"What are you making at Distressed Success?"

She hesitated. "I'm getting around sixty in the shop right now."

He looked impressed. "Superb."

"Location is everything," she allowed. Then emboldened, she decided to put down some qualifications of her own. "You could achieve the same in Sperling stores, but I'd have to be assured of proper product placement—good sight lines, and some swing areas."

"Done...but I need an exclusive deal."

"What kind of exclusive deal?" She tried to read his expression again, but couldn't.

"You partner with me only. No relationships with other parties."

Eleven

She felt a flutter in her stomach, then wet her lips.

His eyes zeroed in on the action and flared, before his eyelids dropped to conceal his expression.

"With an exclusive deal—" she cleared the catch in her voice "—I'd expect…more."

He shifted closer. "Name your terms."

"Are we still talking about Sperling, Inc. and Distressed Success?" she asked, huskily.

The tension was unbearable.

"I don't know," he said, raising his hand to cup the side of her face, his fingers delving into her hair. "Are we?"

"Aren't you worried about partnering with me?"

She searched his eyes. "I am Brenda Hartley's daughter. I even look like her."

"I *like* the way you look." His fingers caressed her scalp, making her want to purr. "And for the record, you're nothing like your mother in the ways that count. You're no more like Brenda because you have red hair and hazel eyes than I'm like Webb because I've become head of Sperling, Inc."

"People may be surprised to hear we've... hooked up," she whispered.

His eyes lowered to her mouth. "We might as well make a big splash."

"We're from different worlds—"

"We're alike, you and I," he contradicted, smiling wryly as his eyes met hers again. "We've both spent our whole lives making sure we *didn't* become our parents."

"You do have a point there," she conceded.

"See," he joked, "that's a great first step—admitting I'm right. I foresee a beautiful...partnership."

Her laugh came out weak and breathless.

He leaned forward and placed light kisses on her nose, the corner of her mouth, her lips....

"You know," she joked, "this is inappropriate...if I'm giving a presentation to become your business partner."

"But not," he responded in a low voice, "if you're interviewing for the position of wife."

Her heart flipped over. "What did you say?"

Instead of responding, he kissed her, long and deep.

When he finally pulled away, he said, "Marry me and let's have kids."

"*Yes.*" Tears pricked the back of her eyes. "I called up Webb last week and told him I was no longer interested in getting my designs into Sperling stores."

"I know," he said quietly, catching a tear with the pad of his thumb.

"*You know?*"

He nodded. "The first thing I did when my ownership became official was to call up the managers at Sperling headquarters and find out where your contract was in the pipeline."

She smiled through her tears. "So you could torpedo it, I would have thought."

He shook his head, his expression wry. "So I could move it along. Imagine my surprise when I found out the negotiations had stalled...at *your* request."

"I wasn't sure you'd believe me if I told you I'd pulled out *before* your takeover became public."

"I would have believed you, because you're too important to me. My *first* order of business was to find out what had happened to your contract." He smiled ruefully. "Imagine how perplexed the people at Sperling were when the new majority owner's first questions were about a contract that most of them had never heard of and that had worked its way down the food chain."

She blinked back tears.

He sobered. "Why did you do it? Why pull out when Sperling was the key to your going national?"

"Pride," she said. "Brenda told me that you'd given her some money."

Ryan cursed under his breath. *"She told you?"*

"Yes."

"And you drew the worst possible conclusion," he guessed.

She nodded. "I wanted to repay you. I didn't want you to think I was some—" her vision got blurry again "—some floozy you could b-buy."

"Aw, honey." He grasped her upper arms and started kissing away tears that had seeped out. "That's not why I did it. I wanted Brenda to go away, so we could concentrate on straightening things out between us. I'd just had the most incredible weekend of my life."

"That's just it," she said, hiccupping. "Your paying off Brenda, coming on the heels of my finding out you'd known all along about my sexual history or lack thereof, made me think that sex was all you wanted from me."

"Honey, if all you want from *me* is sex, I'll die a happy man."

She gave a watery laugh.

He sobered again. "The more I fought against my attraction to you, the more I fell under your spell. It became impossible to ignore how alike we are."

"Two people trying like crazy *not* to be their parents?" she supplied.

Her comment elicited a smile. "Actually, your sexual inexperience made me realize you'd been just as affected, if not more so, by growing up as Brenda Hartley's daughter as I was by being raised as Webb Sperling's son."

"The first guy I slept with was a fellow college student," she supplied. "Then he met Brenda and announced our relationship couldn't possibly go anywhere. He had serious plans to storm the corporate world, and an in-law like Brenda would have been a liability."

"Idiot."

She smiled. "Between that and the sex not being all that terrific to start with, Tyler sort of soured me on relationships for a long time. After growing up with Brenda, it had been a leap of faith for me to get involved with him to begin with."

He nodded. "My parents had an unhappy marriage, and when I arrived in Hunter's Landing, you were the last woman I would have said I'd get involved with. But you made me love you."

"I love you, too," she said shakily.

He leaned in for another kiss, one that quickly turned hot and full of promise.

She pulled him closer, her fingers splaying and delving into his hair as he plundered her mouth.

When they finally broke apart, they both took labored breaths.

"I need—"

"Make—"

They both stopped and Ryan grinned.

"Bed," he said simply.

Somehow, they made it up the stairs and to her bedroom.

She went to him then and stood by the bed, sandwiched between his legs.

He went to work on the buttons of her blouse, kissing each inch of skin as it was exposed.

She sighed and held him to her. Outside, the storm continued to rage, beating against the windows, but inside they were locked in their own world.

He peeled the blouse from her, then gazed into her eyes. "I've been a fervent admirer of your breasts."

She laughed. "I *thought* I saw you looking—"

"It was impossible not to."

"And yet you resisted me."

"It was a losing battle."

Then his mouth nestled in the dark valley created by her cleavage, placing moist kisses there.

Kelly gave a low moan.

When he released the clasp of her bra, her breasts fell into his hands like ripe fruit, tight and firm, and he kneaded them until she felt warmth spread within her.

Her skirt hit the floor next and his hand smoothed up and down the side of her thigh.

"Fantastic legs, too," he murmured.

"Being on my feet all day gives them plenty of exercise," she demurred.

"You're the total package. Beautiful inside and out."

She was sensitized to react to his every word… his every look…his every touch.

He undid his shirt, then stood, and between increasingly passionate kisses, he let her help him off with the rest of his clothing.

Her hand grazed his erection, stoking their need as their breathing became heavy with desire.

Once he'd lowered her panties and she'd stepped out of them along with her slipper-footed mules so that they both were naked, he tumbled her onto the bed next to him and began to caress her.

She arched to his touch, feeling him bringing her to life with every masterful stroke.

When he reached the spot at the juncture of her thighs, her world tilted, her breathing coming in audible gasps.

He licked and she was on fire.

He refused to relent, however, until she trembled and shook against him, cresting on a wave of deliverance and emotion that left her spent and replete at the same time.

He moved next to her then, driving need stamped

on his face, heavy on the scent of his skin and etched in the tension of his muscles.

"Protection," he rasped, looking around at the jumble of his clothes.

"You know I haven't been with anyone since—"

He went still. "It was a long time for me before you and I've been tested."

"Me, too."

"Are you sure?"

Her heart opened. "Would it be so bad if we got started on kids sooner rather than later?"

"Heck, no," he said.

"I want it all," she said, "the career, kids, you." Then there was no talking as he gathered her against him. He positioned himself and slid into her on a wave of mingled moans and sighs, and together they began to ride the wave.

She hung on to him, her hands low on his hips, meeting his thrusts, which sent them higher and higher, until they came at the same time.

She called his name as she felt him groan harshly against her neck.

Afterward, they lay together in bed, hearing the storm wreak its havoc outside.

"I can't believe you drove here in this weather," she said in disbelief.

His hand smoothed up and down her arm. "My month is almost up. I came as soon as I dealt with the fallout from my takeover of Sperling, Inc. I knew I had to resolve what was between us before I left."

"Just think," she responded, "if you hadn't been forced to spend a month at the lodge, we would never have met."

"I didn't come to Hunter's Landing looking for a woman," Ryan said, placing a light kiss on her lips. "In fact, it was the furthest thing from my mind. I was closing in on Webb—just about at the point where I had enough shares lined up to oust him—and I was pissed off about being forced to take off a month to cool my heels."

Kelly turned toward him fully. "Why *were* you set on taking over Sperling, Inc.? I mean, I know you dislike Webb, but—"

"It wasn't just revenge for what he did to my mother, though that was part of it," Ryan admitted. "He was mismanaging the stores, squandering the family heritage."

"And now that you have control, what do you plan to do?" she asked curiously.

"Sperling has been treading water at best under Webb's leadership," he responded. "Sales and profits have been lackluster. I'm planning on taking the stores more upscale and improving customer service. We need to stock cutting-edge fashion. There's no point in trying to beat discount merchants at their own game."

It was exactly what she'd do, Kelly thought, then

realized she shouldn't be surprised by Ryan's business acumen. After all, he was the man who had thumbed his nose at taking his rightful place in the family company and had instead, in ten short years, built one of the most dynamic, profitable cable companies around, buying up competitors for a song and turning them around, in part with the synergies created by his own burgeoning empire.

"So now you're a retail mogul as well as a cable-company tycoon," she teased.

"Yeah," Ryan conceded, "but I'm planning to delegate most of the work for the stores." He arched a brow. "Are you interested in helping?"

Kelly laughed. "I went looking for just an outlet for my designs, and wound up with the whole chain at my disposal."

"Honey, you have *me* at your disposal."

Kelly felt a quiver run through her. "Just a few hours ago, I was sitting on the couch thinking we were over."

He gave her a quick, fiery kiss. "My victory over Webb didn't give me the satisfaction I thought it would. Instead, I spent my time thinking about *you*. Thanks to Hunter's will, I've had time to figure out what's meaningful."

"I wonder if that was Hunter's motive all along," she mused.

"I've wondered the same thing," Ryan admitted. "He knew me and the other guys well. There was no way he could have predicted what our lives would be like ten years on, but maybe he had an inkling, since we were all hard-charging types, that we might need a little incentive to force us to take a breather, to assess how far we'd come and where we were going."

"You mean, he might have had a clue you'd turn into a driven corporate shark?"

"Maybe." He grinned good-naturedly. "I don't know how seriously the rest of us took that pact that we'd made to reunite in ten years. I'd forgotten all about it before my stay at the lodge. Maybe Hunter knew that would happen—that it would be up to him to make sure the Samurai weren't lost forever. Now I can't wait till I see the others. We have a lot to thank Hunter for."

"And thanks to you," Kelly said, "I realized we can't run from our past—"

"—but we can run toward our future, together," he finished for her.

And then there was no more talking, as he showed her exactly what some of their future would hold.

Ryan looked around the lodge one last time. It had been a hell of a month. He'd walked in seeking one thing and he was walking away with something else entirely.

Something better. Purer. Love in an unexpected

package, in an unexpected place. And he was a better person for it.

He sat in the great room, looking out at the midday sun, contemplating the note in front of him. It was part of his plan to begin building bridges to his old college buddies.

"What are you doing?" Kelly said, walking into the room and coming to sit on the arm of his chair.

"Composing a note to Matt Barton." He tapped the top of his pen against the coffee table. "He's due to arrive soon to start his month at the lodge."

Kelly smiled. "Telling him what a wonderful time you had here?"

"This place really is the Love Shack," he responded, then grinned. "All four of the guys who've spent a month here have wound up finding the One. And you know what they say. Forewarned is forearmed."

Kelly swatted him playfully.

They were about to embark on a trip to Napa Valley, where they planned to have an intimate wedding. Then they were heading back to the real world, so he could get back to work at El Ray Technology.

Kelly was already helping him get Sperling, Inc. back on track, offering advice about how the stores could be revamped. She was also placing production orders for her designs, so that they could be found in Sperling stores in the coming months.

Kelly had asked Erica to run Distressed Success for her in the meantime, and had hired a couple of local college students to help out. She wanted to keep the shop open while she expanded nationally.

Kelly leaned forward. "What did you write?"

Ryan picked up the piece of paper and read it aloud: "Matt, good luck, bud. I'm passing on a piece of advice. You're about to begin your month at 'the Love Shack.' Remember the universal truths about women we came up with on New Year's Eve our senior year? They tie you down and won't let you do anything dangerous? Scrap 'em. Here are the new universal truths about the One: She'll set you free. Loving her is the most dangerous thing you'll ever do. Ryan."

"Aww…"

Ryan smiled. "Don't get all weepy on me. Knowing Matt, he'll read it and think it's a load of BS."

Kelly looked at him archly. "I'm surprised there was nothing in your universal truths about sex. You know, seven college guys, lots of testosterone…you must have been thinking about it all the time."

Ryan grinned. "Yeah, well…I didn't want to say the sex *doesn't* get boring. Some things a guy wants to keep to himself."

Kelly slipped off the chair arm and into his lap, looping her arms around his neck. As she pulled his head down to hers, she murmured, "Come here and I'll prove that part to you right now."

"I guess our departure *can* wait," Ryan responded as they set about proving the universal truths they'd both discovered in the last month.

* * * * *

The MILLIONAIRE OF THE MONTH
series continues with
MARRIED TO HIS BUSINESS
by Elizabeth Bevarly,
available July from Silhouette Desire.

THE ROYAL HOUSE OF NIROLI
Always passionate, always proud

The richest royal family in the world—united by
blood and passion, torn apart by deceit and desire

Nestled in the azure blue of the Mediterranean Sea, the
majestic island of Niroli has prospered for centuries.
The Fierezza men have worn the crown with passion and
pride since ancient times. But now, as the king's health
declines, and his two sons have been tragically killed, the
crown is in jeopardy.

The clock is ticking—a new heir must be found
before the king is forced to abdicate. By royal decree
the internationally scattered members of the Fierezza
family are summoned to claim their destiny. But any
person who takes the throne must do so according to
The Rules of the Royal House of Niroli. Soon secrets
and rivalries emerge as the descendents of this ancient
royal line vie for position and power. Only a true
Fierezza can become ruler—a person dedicated to their
country, their people…and their eternal love!

Each month starting in July 2007,
Harlequin Presents is delighted to bring you
an exciting installment from
THE ROYAL HOUSE OF NIROLI,
in which you can follow the epic search for
the true Nirolian king.
Eight heirs, eight romances, eight fantastic stories!

Here's your chance to enjoy a sneak preview of the
first book delivered to you by royal decree…

FIVE minutes later she was standing immobile in front of the study's window, her original purpose of coming in forgotten, as she stared in shocked horror at the envelope she was holding. Waves of heat followed by icy chill surged through her body. She could hardly see the address now through her blurred vision, but the crest on its left-hand front corner stood out, its *royal* crest, followed by the address: *HRH Prince Marco of Niroli…*

She didn't hear Marco's key in the apartment door, she didn't even hear him calling out her name. Her shock was so great that nothing could penetrate it. It encased her in a kind of bubble, which only concentrated the torment of what she was suffering and branded it on her brain so that it could never be forgotten. It was only finally pierced by the sudden opening of the study door as Marco walked in.

"Welcome home, *Your Highness*. I suppose I ought to curtsy." She waited, praying that he would laugh and tell her that she had got it all wrong, that the envelope she was holding, addressing him as Prince Marco of Niroli, was some silly mistake. But like a tiny candle flame shivering vulnerably in the dark, her hope trembled fearfully. And then the look in Marco's eyes extinguished it as cruelly as a hand placed callously over a dying person's face to stem their last breath.

"Give that to me," he demanded, taking the envelope from her.

"It's too late, Marco," Emily told him brokenly. "I know the truth now…." She dug her teeth in her lower lip to try to force back her own pain.

"You had no right to go through my desk," Marco shot back at her furiously, full of loathing at being caught off-guard and forced into a position in which he was in the wrong, making him determined to find something he could accuse Emily of. "I trusted you…."

Emily could hardly believe what she was hearing. "No, you didn't trust me, Marco, and you didn't trust me because you knew that I couldn't trust you. And you knew that because you're a liar, and liars don't trust people because they know that they themselves cannot be trusted." She not only felt sick, she also felt as though she could hardly breathe. "You are Prince Marco of Niroli…. How could you not tell me who you are and still live with me as intimately as we have lived together?" she demanded brokenly.

"Stop being so ridiculously dramatic," Marco demanded fiercely. "You are making too much of the situation."

"*Too much?*" Emily almost screamed the words at him. "When were you going to tell me, Marco? Perhaps you just planned to walk away without telling me anything? After all, what do my feelings matter to you?"

"Of course they matter." Marco stopped her sharply. "And it was in part to protect them, and you, that I decided not to inform you when my grandfather first announced that he intended to step down from the throne and hand it on to me."

"To protect me?" Emily nearly choked on her fury. "Hand on the throne? No wonder you told me when you first took me to bed that all you wanted was sex. You *knew* that was the only kind of relationship there could ever be between us! You *knew* that one day you would be Niroli's king. No doubt you are expected to marry a princess. Is she picked out for you already, your *royal* bride?"

* * * * *

Look for
THE FUTURE KING'S PREGNANT MISTRESS
by Penny Jordan in July 2007,
from Harlequin Presents,
available wherever books are sold.

Mediterranean NIGHTS™

Experience the glamour and elegance of cruising the high seas with a new 12-book series....

MEDITERRANEAN NIGHTS

Coming in July 2007...

SCENT OF A WOMAN

by

Joanne Rock

When Danielle Chevalier is invited to an exclusive conference aboard *Alexandra's Dream,* she knows it will mean good things for her struggling fragrance company. But her dreams get a setback when she meets Adam Burns, a representative from a large American conglomerate.

Danielle is charmed by the brusque American— until she finds out he means to compete with her bid for the opportunity that will save her family business!

Silhouette®

Romantic
SUSPENSE

**Sparked by Danger,
Fueled by Passion.**

Mission: Impassioned

A brand-new miniseries begins with

My Spy

By *USA TODAY* bestselling author

Marie Ferrarella

She had to trust him with her life....
It was the most daring mission of Joshua Lazlo's
career: rescuing the prime minister of England's
daughter from a gang of cold-blooded kidnappers.
But nothing prepared the shadowy secret agent
for a fiery woman whose touch ignited something
far more dangerous.

My Spy

#1472

Available July 2007 wherever you buy books!

nocturne™

**DON'T MISS THE RIVETING CONCLUSION
TO THE RAINTREE TRILOGY**

RAINTREE: SANCTUARY

by *New York Times* bestselling author

BEVERLY
BARTON

Mercy, guardian of the Raintree
homeplace, takes a stand against
the Ansara wizards to battle for
the Clan's future.

*On sale July,
wherever books are sold.*

SNRT2

REQUEST YOUR FREE BOOKS!

2 FREE NOVELS PLUS 2 FREE GIFTS!

Passionate, Powerful, Provocative!

YES! Please send me 2 FREE Silhouette Desire® novels and my 2 FREE gifts. After receiving them, if I don't wish to receive any more books, I can return the shipping statement marked "cancel." If I don't cancel, I will receive 6 brand-new novels every month and be billed just $3.80 per book in the U.S., or $4.47 per book in Canada, plus 25¢ shipping and handling per book and applicable taxes, if any*. That's a savings of almost 15% off the cover price! I understand that accepting the 2 free books and gifts places me under no obligation to buy anything. I can always return a shipment and cancel at any time. Even if I never buy another book from Silhouette, the two free books and gifts are mine to keep forever.

225 SDN EEXJ   326 SDN EEXU

Name	(PLEASE PRINT)	
Address		Apt.
City	State/Prov.	Zip/Postal Code

Signature (if under 18, a parent or guardian must sign)

Mail to the **Silhouette Reader Service™:**
IN U.S.A.: P.O. Box 1867, Buffalo, NY 14240-1867
IN CANADA: P.O. Box 609, Fort Erie, Ontario L2A 5X3

Not valid to current Silhouette Desire subscribers.

Want to try two free books from another line?
Call 1-800-873-8635 or visit www.morefreebooks.com.

* Terms and prices subject to change without notice. NY residents add applicable sales tax. Canadian residents will be charged applicable provincial taxes and GST. This offer is limited to one order per household. All orders subject to approval. Credit or debit balances in a customer's account(s) may be offset by any other outstanding balance owed by or to the customer. Please allow 4 to 6 weeks for delivery.

Your Privacy: Silhouette is committed to protecting your privacy. Our Privacy Policy is available online at www.eHarlequin.com or upon request from the Reader Service. From time to time we make our lists of customers available to reputable firms who may have a product or service of interest to you. If you would prefer we not share your name and address, please check here. ☐

SDES07

THE ROYAL HOUSE OF NIROLI

Always passionate, always proud.

**The richest royal family in the world—
a family united by blood and passion,
torn apart by deceit and desire.**

Step into the glamorous, enticing world of the
Nirolian Royal Family. As the king ails he must find an
heir…each month an exciting new installment follows
the epic search for the true Nirolian king. Eight heirs,
eight romances, eight fantastic stories!

It's time for playboy prince Marco Fierezza to
claim his rightful place…on the throne of Niroli!
Emily loves Marco, but she has no idea he's a royal
prince! What will this king-in-waiting do when he
discovers his mistress is pregnant?

THE FUTURE KING'S
PREGNANT MISTRESS

by Penny Jordan

(#2643)

On sale July 2007.

SPECIAL EDITION™

Look for six new MONTANA MAVERICKS stories, beginning in July with

THE MAN WHO HAD EVERYTHING

by *CHRISTINE RIMMER*

When Grant Clifton decided to sell the family ranch, he knew it would devastate Stephanie Julen, the caretaker who'd always been like a little sister to him. He wanted a new start, but how could he tell her that she and her mother would have to leave...especially now that he was head over heels in love with her?

MONTANA MAVERICKS

Dreaming big—and winning hearts—in Big Sky Country

COMING NEXT MONTH

#1807 THE CEO'S SCANDALOUS AFFAIR—
Roxanne St. Claire
Dynasties: The Garrisons
He needed her for just one night—but the repercussions of their sensual evening could last a lifetime!

#1808 HIGH-SOCIETY MISTRESS—Katherine Garbera
The Mistresses
He will stop at nothing to take over his business rival's company…including bedding his enemy's daughter and making her his mistress.

#1809 MARRIED TO HIS BUSINESS—Elizabeth Bevarly
Millionaire of the Month
To get his assistant back this CEO plans to woo and seduce her. But he isn't prepared when she ups the stakes on *his* game.

#1810 THE PRINCE'S ULTIMATE DECEPTION—
Emilie Rose
Monte Carlo Affairs
It was a carefree vacation romance. Until she discovers she's having an affair with a prince in disguise.

#1811 ROSSELLINI'S REVENGE AFFAIR—
Yvonne Lindsay
He blamed her for his family's misery and sought revenge in a most passionate way!

#1812 THE BOSS'S DEMAND—Jennifer Lewis
She was pregnant with the boss's baby—but wanted more than just the convenient marriage he was offering.

SDCNM0607